Love Hertz

SILVER HILLS COZY MYSTERIES, Volume 9

Sam Cheever

Published by Electric Prose Publications, 2023.

LOVE HERTZ

First edition. January 12, 2023.

Written by Sam Cheever.

COME TO SILVER HILLS. *Where making friends can prove deadly and creating enemies might be easier than you think.*

Emotions are aflutter at Silver Hills as a new heartthrob moves into the residence. Will all that fluttering still a single heart? And if love dies, will Flo's very own *amour* find itself in the crosshairs of the estimable Detective Brent Peters?

Agnes and Hertz are on the outs. Secrets tear the tender fabric of a pulsing heart. What do the secrets have to do with murder?

Affairs of *le cœur* aside, will Agnes break the clothing store shopping for a party dress? What will break during a rousing class of Zumba? And will Flo be able to soldier through her dance injuries to follow a chubby cherub to a killer?

So many questions. So much hopping, tapping and fluttering. And still a murder to solve.

What will Flo and Co. do?

They'll do what they always do, of course. Hearts out and chins up, they're goin' in!

Sam doesn't give away a lot of books. But she values her readers and, to show it, she's gifting you a copy of a fun book just for signing up for her newsletter!
<u>SIGN UP HERE!</u>[1]

---

1. https://samcheever.com/newsletter/

https://samcheever.com/newsletter/

CHAPTER ONE

"Come on, Flo. I've seen ants that can lift more than that."

Flo glared at her friend, her muscles quivering under the strain of the metal weights. "I'm gonna lift these right up to your head if you don't stop razzing me," she told Agnes.

"I'm not razzing. I'm motivating."

Climbing a virtual mountain in a digital headwind on a nearby stationary bike, Celia Angonetti snorted. "Apparently, Agnes went to the Marine Drill Sargent school of motivation."

Flo shook her head. "I'm not a fan of that motivational style, Agnes," she told her friend. "If you don't stop, I'm going to show you some motivation with one of these weights."

Agnes rolled her gray eyes. "Fine. Then let me try a different style." She curved her lips into a fake smile. "I'm definitely seeing some improvement, Flo. I think your arms are looking less baby-bird-like and more like stalks of anemic celery."

With a groan, Flo handed the weights to Agnes, pushing herself into a sitting position on the bench. She shoved fingers into her newly styled, light-brown bouff, trying to fluff it up again. "I can't tell you how motivated that makes me feel," she told Agnes. "Thanks so much."

"You're welcome." Agnes placed the seven-pound weights back into the holder. "I was going to ask you to spot me while I lift, but you'd probably drop the weights on my head with those spindly girl arms."

Growling under her breath, Flo swiped a towel over her glistening face. "What's got your bloomers in a twist this morning, Agnes? Did you accidentally eat a raisin in your oatmeal?"

She grimaced. "Not a chance. I can smell those wrinkly disasters a mile away."

When a frown continued to blossom on her friend's wide face, Flo tried again. "What is it?"

Agnes glanced at Celia, who'd conquered the peak of the virtual mountain and was happily spinning downward, her slender form bathed in sweat and a smile on her face.

Agnes led Flo away from their friend. "It's Hertz. He's thinking about moving out of Silver Hills."

Hertz was Agnes' new boyfriend. The two of them had become almost inseparable of late. To the point where Flo kind of missed spending time with her friend. It didn't help that things had been really slow in her private investigation business. Nobody'd tried to hire her for a couple of months.

Flo was getting antsy. "Why? I thought he loved it here."

"He does." Agnes skimmed the graying brown strands of her chin-length pageboy behind her ears. She grabbed a twenty-pound weight from the stand and proceeded to work a muscular right arm as she spoke to Flo. "I think it's a money thing, but I can't get him to talk to me about it."

"Oh, dear," Flo said. "I'm so sorry, Agnes. I'd be sad to see him go. But just because he moves out of Silver Hills doesn't mean you can't still see each other."

"I know. But it just won't be the same." She switched the weight to her other hand and repeated the reps on that arm.

"Do you want me to talk to Richard?"

Richard Attles was the day manager at Silver Hills. He was also Roger Attles' son and, since Roger and Flo were a bit of an item themselves, she had some influence over Richard. "Maybe there's a studio apartment coming available. "The studios were very popular and there were rarely vacancies for one. But they did have one they used for display purposes. "Maybe he could move into a display if he agreed to let the managers show it when they had an interested party."

Agnes settled the weight back into the holder, her frown softening. "That's not a bad idea. He can save a thousand a month if he switches to a studio." Her brow furrowed again. "But I know he loves living in his dad's old place. He might not want to move."

Hertz had lost his father a few months earlier, and he'd kept his dad's apartment. Flo thought it was mostly because he wanted to stay close to Agnes. The two of them had hit it off immediately, bonding over their love of food, movies, and cats. "We can give it a try. I'll talk to Roger about it before we go to Richard. Roger and Hertz have gotten pretty close. He might have some idea what's going on there."

Agnes nodded, still looking worried. "Thanks, Flo."

"Of course, hun." Flo gave her a smile. "But you don't look any happier."

Agnes grabbed the towel she'd draped around the back of her neck and dried her face with it. "I need to get going. Hertz and I are going to a movie tonight."

Celia joined them, her own towel clutched in one hand and her pretty face aglow from her efforts. "Are you going to see that *Clue* remake? I'm trying to get Mass to go with me to see it, but he says trying to figure out who offed someone was too much like his day job to be fun."

Massimo Angonetti was Celia's sort-of-estranged gangster husband. They were still married but lived separately. Most likely to give Celia plausible deniability with Mass' career. He'd technically never gotten busted by PoPo for doing anything illegal, but his partial fingerprints were probably all over a hundred different crime scenes.

"No," Agnes frowned. "We're going to see a science fiction film." Her lips curled slightly. He knows I hate those," she murmured.

Watching her, Flo wondered what was really bothering her friend. "Why don't you tell him you aren't interested in going to that movie then?"

Agnes shrugged. "I'll see you guys later."

Watching Agnes' six-foot-tall form shuffle out of the gym, worry settled into Flo's belly with the weight of an overbaked scone.

"Trouble in paradise?" Ce asked, slipping her arm through Flo's.

"Could be," Flo agreed. "I sure hope not, though. Agnes has been so happy since Hertz moved into Silver Hills."

"She won't talk about it?" Ce grabbed her water bottle and they headed toward the door.

"Not yet. But I'm not done pestering her. If there's something I can do to help them I want to do it."

Holding the door, Ce nodded. "I'll offer her two free dinners to *Gioppino's* for a Saturday night. That's the night the new Jazz quartet plays. A little candlelight and romantic music might help."

Flo squeezed Ce's arm against her side. "You're the best, Ce. That might be just the ticket."

"There you are, doll."

Flo turned at the sound of Roger Attles' voice. She smiled when she saw him, shoving self-consciously at her bouff where it had been mashed against the weight bench. "Hey, Roger."

Flo slid her smile toward the man he was walking with. "Hello."

"Well hello, beautiful." The man had steel-gray hair, close-cropped and dense on his well-shaped head, and quicksilver gray eyes to match. His startling gaze was enhanced by a thick fringe of black lashes and strong eyebrows that slashed dramatically across his tanned face.

He was almost as tall as Roger but built like an athlete, where Roger was built like a lawyer.

"Doll, this is Nicholai Pearce. He just moved into Silver Hills."

The other man nodded. "I've been staying at a motel just outside of town for a couple of months while I looked for the perfect place to live," he clarified. "I'm thrilled I was able to grab an apartment here at Silver Hills. It's not an easy place to get into."

"It is very popular," she agreed smiling. It's so nice to meet you, Nicholai," Flo shook his hand.

He bent over her hand and placed a kiss on the back, drawing a frown from Roger. "Call me Nic, please. And the pleasure is all mine, Flo."

He said her name like a caress, making her cheeks heat.

"If you'll excuse me. I have a thing..."

Flo turned in surprise to watch Celia walk away, her strides brisk. That was strange. Celia was usually one of the first to greet new residents. Flo flushed with embarrassment. "I'm sorry, she...um...had a thing. How are you enjoying Silver Hills so far?" Flo asked Nic, noting the way his dark brows had lowered as he watched Ce leave.

"It's just great, Flo. The people have been so kind." He tore his gaze from Celia's retreat and pounded Roger on the back, grinning widely. "Old Roger here has already invited me to poker night. Everyone's been so welcoming, I feel as if I've lived here all my life."

"You obviously haven't met the vampires yet, then," Flo joked.

When Nic frowned in confusion, she glanced at Roger. "You haven't warned him about Vlad and Morty?"

"I didn't want to scare him away, doll. It's only his second day in the residence."

Flo laughed. "Well, make sure you fill him in." She grinned. "How does your wife enjoy it so far? I'd love to meet her."

Nic looked at the gold band on his finger, frowning. "I'm afraid I lost her last year."

He looked so miserable, Flo wanted to kick herself. "Oh, I'm so sorry."

"Not your fault. You didn't know. It's actually one of the reasons I moved here. I got tired of bumbling around in that big house all by myself. I thought it would be good for me to be around more people."

"Well, you've definitely come to the right place then," Flo laughed. "You just got yourself a couple hundred nosy neighbors."

"I'm looking forward to getting to know my neighbors better," Nic said, his voice warm. "Much better."

She realized with a start that he was flirting with her. Flo stood in stunned silence for a long moment, unsure how to respond. Finally, Roger cleared his throat. "Well, we're going to be late for poker." He reached over and took Flo's hand, kissing her on the cheek in a maneuver Flo couldn't help reading as marking his territory. "I'll see you later, doll."

"It was nice meeting you," she said awkwardly to Nic. Then she hurried toward the stairs that led down to her apartment on the second floor. Anxious to put some space between herself and their new neighbor. Something about the man bothered her. It wasn't just that he was an outrageous flirt. Although she'd always hated that in a man. It was that he'd flirted with her right in front of Roger when it seemed pretty clear that they were an item.

Celia's response to Nicholai Pearce had been strange. And really out of character for her friend, who was usually very welcoming.

Flo decided she needed to find Ce and ask her about her reaction to the new resident.

"Mrs. Bee?"

She jolted to a stop at the familiar voice, turning to find Hertz Thomson striding quickly in her direction. "Can I speak with you for a moment?"

Flo frowned, not wanting to get in the middle of Agnes' and Hertz's relationship issues. "Of course." She smiled as he stopped in front of her, saying a silent prayer that he just wanted to ask her about something non-relationship related.

Unfortunately, luck was not Flo's lady at the moment.

"I'm glad I caught you," Hertz said, his gaze skimming the area as if looking for someone. "I wanted to talk to you about Agnes..."

Flo held up a hand. "Let me stop you right there, Mr. Thomson..."

"Hertz, please."

"If you'll call me Flo."

He smiled. "Flo. I'm sorry to bother you. I promise I'm not trying to put you in the middle. It's just..." His face folded into a frown, frustration oozing off him. "You know Agnes better than almost anyone."

"I'd like to think I do," she told him. "But she doesn't discuss her relationships with me."

He nodded. "I get that. This is a more...general...question." He twined his hands together, skimming another glance around the floor.

"Out with it, Hertz," Flo said, her tone firm but not unkind. She did feel for him. Romance was hard under the best circumstances, and dealing with a woman who'd spent most of her life alone couldn't be a picnic in the park.

"I need some advice on how to get Agnes to understand why I'm moving."

Flo was caught off guard and said the first thing that popped into her mind. "She thinks you're dumping her."

He expelled air. "I knew it."

"Are you saying that you're not dumping her? Because, if you are, then you should be talking to her, not me."

He shook his head. "I wish it was that simple."

Flo raised her brows, her temper flaring.

He seemed to understand his mistake right away. "That didn't come out the way I meant it. What I'm trying to say is..." He sighed. "I really care for Agnes..."

Flo could hear the "but" coming a mile away. She lifted a hand to stop him. "Nope. I'm not interested in your excuses, Mr. Thomson. Agnes is a wonderful woman. You're lucky that she cares for you. If you intend to break her heart, my advice is to do it quickly and get out of her life so she can pick up the pieces." Flo turned away, her footsteps heavy on the carpet.

She pressed her lips together to keep from giving the younger man what for and hurried to her apartment, hoping to lock herself inside before her mouth opened and spewed all the ugliness her mind was thinking about him.

Flo embraced her anger as she pushed inside, sidestepping her eager, bouncing dachshund as she closed the door firmly behind her.

Rodney needed to go outside and potty, but she wanted to make sure Hertz Thomson had vacated the hallway before she went back out there. Flo didn't trust herself not to smack the man upside the head if she saw him again.

CHAPTER TWO

The next morning, Flo decided to take a walk into town with Rodney. The exercise would be good for both of them, and Flo needed to escape with her thoughts. Her world felt shaky and foreign to her at the moment. With Agnes unhappy, Ce acting strangely, and Nicholai Pearce upsetting the apple cart of her and Roger's relationship, she felt a bit off balance and jittery.

The walk turned out to be a great idea. It didn't take her long to start to feel better. She was soon smiling at Rodney's irrepressible *joie de vie*. It was a bright, sunny early December day but there was no wind and the sun made the low fifties temperature feel more like mid-sixties. It was pleasant enough bundled in her favorite long wool coat and scarf.

Barking happily, his entire backend wiggling with excitement, Rodney was trying to jump up to peek at a litter of kittens in the pet store window when Flo heard a shout. She turned to look across the street but saw only a young woman who looked vaguely familiar, standing in front of the new restaurant across the street. The woman appeared to be in her early forties, with dark red hair and the pale skin that told Flo the hair color was natural. She was dressed in running gear, spandex leggings and a jacket that fit loose enough to give her a good range of movement. She wore her long hair down, flowing over narrow shoulders, and her hands were encased in fingerless gloves. As Flo noticed her, the woman plucked a set of earbuds from her ears and poked a button on her cell as she looked expectantly toward a green area nearby.

Flo was trying to remember where she'd seen the woman before when a man strolled into view. He'd come through a small park with overgrown bushes that Flo recognized as the outdoor seating for the new French Café in warmer climes.

Nicholai Pearce's handsome face looked unhappy, his features tense, and the dark slash of brows were lowered over eyes that Flo imagined glittered with the anger evident in his tautly held frame.

Riveted by their behavior, Flo found herself staring at the couple. Rodney bounced against her leg as he continued to harass the kittens through the glass. She felt her alarm rise as Nic stepped close, one big hand clenching into a fist as he bent toward the red-haired woman, his jaw clenched.

The woman seemed determined to hold her own. She reached to poke him on the shoulder with one finger, earning herself a small reprieve from his hovering as Nic straightened. Their voices rose, drifting across the street toward Flo.

Unfortunately, she couldn't hear what they were fighting about. It looked like a lover's spat. The woman gave Pearce a final poke with a slender digit and then stepped around him, heading down the street with quick, angry strides.

Her identity suddenly dropped into place. Flo didn't know her name, but she was pretty sure the young woman lived on the singles side of Silver Hills.

Had Nicholai Pearce moved into the residence to be closer to the red-haired woman? Had Flo just witnessed a lover's spat? Or was Nic pressing his attentions on another woman who wasn't interested?

Flo's mind churned with questions as she turned back to find Nic staring right at her, his expression hard. She blinked, twitching backward as if struck and then started up the sidewalk again, feeling foolish for being caught gawking.

And even worse, for pretending she hadn't been. When it was clear she'd been staring at the couple the entire time.

FLO AND RODNEY WERE heading into the third-floor library when Elisa Kemp hailed her from outside the elevator.

Elisa hurried up to Flo as she stopped to wait. Rodney licked cookie crumbs from the weekly book club snack off the carpet, his tail happily wagging.

"Flo! I'm so glad to have caught you." Elisa fairly vibrated with whatever news she'd carried down the hall. Her brows lifted as she leaned conspiratorially close. "Have you met our new resident?"

Flo managed not to grimace. "You mean Mr. Pearce?"

Elisa nodded enthusiastically. "Word is he lost his wife recently."

"Yes. He told me it was last year. Do you know how she died?" Flo hated to indulge in gossip, but the scene on the street had piqued her interest in Mr. Nicholai Pearce

"She was murdered. That poor, lovely man was out of the country dealing with a family matter when she was attacked and killed. Apparently, it was a robbery gone bad." Elisa said, ghoulishly happy about the whole thing.

"I don't remember hearing about the murder," Flo said, frowning thoughtfully. She'd have to ask Roger about it. As a lawyer, he paid attention to anything with legal undertones in the city.

"Ah, it didn't happen here. It was in Indianapolis."

"That's terrible," Flo said. "Poor man."

Elisa quivered with happiness. "Yes!"

Flo's poor opinion of the man softened a bit. Maybe he wasn't as bad as she'd thought he was. Some men just couldn't help playing the Banty rooster around women. She determined to give him another chance the next time she ran into him.

"There was some speculation that he was involved," Elisa said. She leaned close, head mere inches from Flo's. "He was having an affair," she said in a harsh whisper.

Okay, maybe her instincts about the man had been spot on. "Really? Was there money involved?" Murder was generally motivated by money, love, or retribution. Flo's experience was that the first two often came together. A deadly two-some.

Elisa shook her head. "I don't know. I'm still trying to ferret that out."

Despite herself, Flo was interested. She knew she shouldn't indulge Elisa's gossiping ways, but she couldn't seem to stop herself from asking, "Will you keep me updated on that?"

Elisa nodded enthusiastically. "See you around, Flo."

Flo said goodbye to the gossip queen and headed toward the bookshelves, intending to grab a new mystery novel to read. Rodney bounced along in front of her, his tail wagging.

Roger called out as she searched the shelves. She turned to find him stepping out of the elevator with a small box in his hands.

"Hey, doll. I'm glad I ran into you. Do you still want this antique tea set I've been storing in the basement?"

Flo eyed the slightly damp box in his hands. The faint scent of mildew hit her senses, making her nose crinkle. "I'd love it. Unfortunately, I took stock of my kitchen space, and I don't really have room for it. Why? Are you in a hurry to get rid of it?"

He shook his head. "Not at all. But, you're aware that I put a flyer on the bulletin board in the hall?"

She nodded.

"Well, I'm determined to clean out all that stuff downstairs. It's just that one of the young women on the singles side was interested in the set. I don't have to sell it to her if you still want it. Just say the word."

She patted his arm. "No, you go ahead and sell it. I won't use it enough to make it worth buying and storing. It's a beautiful set. It would be a shame for it not to be used and appreciated."

"I figured you'd say that. I'm heading over there now to do the deal. Would you like to come with?"

Flo fought the frown trying to transform her face. "I don't know. I was planning on making myself some tea and curling up with TC's latest mystery." Flo's friend, Tricia Colombo, was Activity Director at Silver Hills as well as a popular mystery author.

Roger waggled his brows. "Did our girl put any S-E-X in this one?"

Flo blew air softly through her lips. "No, TC hasn't succumbed to Agnes' pressure. And she never will. A, she's much too stubborn. And, B, her mother reads her books. She'll never go steamy as long as that's the case."

Roger chuckled, his gaze lifting toward the end of the hall. "Oh, there's my potential buyer now. Are you sure you don't want to come with me?"

Flo turned to find the redhead she'd seen arguing with Nic Pearce turning the key in her door at the very end of the hall. "Oh. That's her? Yes. I think I would like to come with you after all, Roger."

"Miss Caldone?" Roger called out as the woman started to enter her apartment. She stopped, turning a frown in their direction. The frown slid away when she saw Flo and Roger. "Oh, hello." She smiled. "Can I help you?"

Flo returned the smile, offering the woman her hand. "I'm Flo Bee. I think you've met Roger?"

The woman shook her head, giving their hands a quick shake. "Only by phone. My name's Mae. How are you?"

Roger lifted the moldy box. "I brought the tea set for you to look at. If you think you'd like it, I have a serving set that matches. They belonged to my mother."

The woman looked into the box, pushing a damp flap aside to peruse the contents. "It's so pretty." Her gaze was alight when she looked up at him. "I'm definitely interested. Would you like to come inside?"

"Yes. Thank you," Roger responded, giving Flo a wink behind the younger woman's back.

The apartment was a studio, basically one large room with a small kitchenette and a single, oversized bathroom. The woman had made the most of the limited space, filling it with a cozy mix of modern furnishings and antiques, and adding a colorful array of artwork to give character to the white walls.

She placed her purse down on a small desk in the center of the longest wall. "I don't have much as far as refreshments. I can offer you coffee or a bottle of water."

They shook their heads. "We won't keep you," Roger said. "I just wanted to show you the set."

Flo looked around as Roger pulled all the pieces of the tea set from the box, and the woman examined each carefully. Flo hadn't been lying about deciding against taking the set because of limited kitchen space. The red-haired woman had even less space than Flo's. She wondered where the woman would put it.

"Good!" Roger said enthusiastically. "I'll bring the other things back later then. We can settle up on all of it then."

They shook hands and Flo turned to the woman. "I believe I saw you downtown earlier. You struck me as familiar. I'm thinking we passed in the Silver Hills dining room at some point."

The woman laughed good-naturedly. "Probably." She indicated the tiny kitchen with a swing of her hand. "As you can see, I don't really use a kitchen. I eat out or just nibble."

Flo gave her a knowing smile. "Don't like to cook?"

"No. But that's only part of it. When I got my divorce, I promised myself I'd never cook a meal against my will again." Her lips twisted briefly. "And why would I, when Cook is such a connoisseur of the culinary arts?" All bitterness left her expression as she smiled.

"She is, isn't she?" The woman had apparently survived a bad marriage, which made the scene on the street with Nic

Pearce seem even more unsettling. "If you don't mind my asking, what are you planning to do with the tea set?"

Mae nodded. "Fair question. It's actually a gift for my sister. She loves antiques and all things tea." Her laughter was pure, genuine. "They're for Christmas."

"Ah." Flo searched for a way to bring up the scene she'd witnessed downtown. "She's going to love it. I saw you outside that new French café downtown. Have you eaten there yet? I've been dying to try it."

Something dark flicked through her green gaze. She chased it away and shook her head. "No. Haven't been there yet. But I'm anxious to try it too."

Roger's cell phone rang. He glanced at the screen. "I need to take this, ladies. I'll be just out in the hall, doll."

Flo nodded, watching him leave before turning back to Mae. "I couldn't help noticing that you had a bit of a disagreement with Nicholai Pearce. Is everything...okay?" Flo asked quietly.

A quick flash of anger slipped across the woman's features and then slid away. She sighed. "Yes. He's just getting a little too possessive and domineering," Mae admitted. "We've only gone out a few times. I went through that once with my ex and I'm not going through it again. I broke it off with him. He isn't taking it too well."

"He didn't threaten you, did he, hun?"

"Not really. He's just refusing to leave me alone." She sighed. "I might have to get a restraining order against him. I hate to do it. It's going to be hard to avoid him here at Silver Hills over the next few weeks."

When Flo cocked her head in silent question, Mae explained. "I'm moving out at the end of the month."

"I'm sorry to hear that," Flo said. "You're not happy here?"

"It's fine, I just..." She shook her head and forced a smile. "Anyway, thanks for your concern. But I don't expect that Nicholai Pearce is going to be a problem for me much longer."

Flo nodded. "You knew about his wife? That she was killed?"

"I did. He told me about it on our first date." She laughed. "It's a wonder we ever had a second date."

"I'm sure he's still reeling from that," Flo said.

"If he is, he hides it well. He's a player," Mae said, giving Flo an earnest look. "Keep your distance from him, Flo. And keep your friends away too. Nicholai Pearce is nothing but trouble. Believe me, I know. I'm drawn to his type like bees to pollen."

I said goodbye to Mae and rejoined Roger in the hall just as he was hanging up his phone. He was frowning.

"Is everything okay?" Flo asked him.

"Everything's perfect, doll," he responded, though the smile on his lips didn't quite reach his eyes. "Arthur just needs my help with something. I'll head over there now. Can I walk you back to your place first?"

"No, I'm fine. But thanks. You go help Arthur." Arthur Janick was Roger's old partner at *Janick, Attles, and Benedick*, the Silver City-based law firm they'd built together.

"I'll see you in the morning? Maybe we could take a walk through the park. I heard we have a new pair of swans on the lake."

"I'd love that. I'll talk to you at breakfast."

CHAPTER THREE

"It won't be so bad, Agnes," TC said, patting her friend's hand where it rested on the table. "It would be nice to have a dressy dress in case you want to go somewhere nice in the future."

Agnes grimaced, clearly not buying what TC was selling.

"Morning!" Flo greeted her friends as she pulled out a chair. "How is everybody today?"

Agnes grunted. Judging by her sour face, she'd been better.

"What's wrong?" Flo asked, looking to TC since Agnes tended to go quiet when she was unhappy.

"Agnes needs to go shopping for a dress. Hertz invited her to his sister's engagement party."

Flo grinned. "Is that all? I thought somebody had died, judging by the look on Agnes' face."

"Something *is* going to die," Agnes groused. "My soul. I'd rather be dead than go shopping."

"Don't be silly, hun." Flo waved to Celia as she made her way through the tables. "It'll be fun. I'll go with you. We'll do lunch and make a day of it."

TC nodded. "Me too. I don't have any events scheduled for today. I've earned a little *me* time."

As Activities Director at Silver Hills, TC was in charge of providing fun and invigorating events at the residence.

"I'd think you'd be gearing up for Christmas by now," Flo told her. She flagged down her favorite waitress, Becky, with a wave and a smile.

Celia yanked a chair out and dropped into it as if she'd just run a marathon. "Land sakes, I thought I'd never get to this chair."

Flo looked at her friend, her eyes widening. Celia was a delicate beauty, pure class and elegance unless she was ripening the air around her during yoga class. She was always perfectly coiffed and dressed in classy, simple clothes, every silky strand of her smooth, blonde bob in place. To say that she wasn't in her usual state of near perfection was an understatement of gargantuan proportions.

"What in the world happened to you?" Flo asked, eyeing Celia's disheveled hair, smeared makeup, and crooked and stained clothing.

"Mass happened to me," she said, groaning.

Flo threw up her hands. "No details, please!"

Even Celia's laugh was worn around the edges. "It's not what you think. He's decided he wants to update the restaurant. He's had me climbing over furniture and crawling around on the floor, measuring stuff and cataloging repairs we need to do. I'm exhausted."

"I know just the thing to perk you right up," TC told Ce grinning. "We're all going shopping to find Agnes a party dress."

Ce's blue gaze widened. "Really? Oh, I'm in, Sisters. That sounds like tons of fun."

Agnes grumbled again.

Becky hurried over, pink-cheeked and apologetic. "I'm so sorry, Mrs. Bee. It's been a crazy morning."

"It's the waffles," Agnes said, the hint of a smile curving itself across her face. "Cook makes the world's best waffles. People come here from all over the city on waffle days."

Becky nodded, rubbing the back of her hand over her forehead. "It's true. I almost dread them."

Flo ordered toast and coffee. Ce ordered coffee and grapefruit juice. When Becky had gone off to get their orders, Flo patted Agnes on a meaty hand. "How about if we try that new French Café for lunch," she bribed, telling herself she didn't have an ulterior motive for going there.

Agnes' shoulders straightened and her face lit up. "Oh yeah. I'll face the death of my soul for that."

Celia laughed, shoving at her messy hair. "With that to look forward to, I might even manage to forget about that fuzzy lump of unidentifiable something I accidentally squashed my hand down on this morning when I was crawling around on the floor."

"Ugh!" TC said in commiseration. "Old, forgotten food?"

Celia shuddered. "I didn't stick around to examine it. Rest assured, Mass is getting an exterminator in today. Just in case."

Her good nature restored, Agnes waggled her brows. "Is the exterminator's name Guido? Is he gonna break the thing's legs?"

"Har," Celia said, her eyes sparkling with good humor. "A good gangster joke never gets old, does it?"

"DOES THIS COME WITH a space helmet?" Agnes asked, her beefy arms held out to her sides and her expression filled with horror.

Flo and TC pressed their lips together, but Celia snorted out a laugh. "Maybe the silver wasn't a good choice."

Agnes stood in front of the three-way mirror, tugging at the ruched side seam of the asymmetrical cocktail dress. The high side of the hem hit her two inches above a wide, dimpled knee, and the long side stuck out a couple of inches below the other knee. The neckline was also asymmetrical and it was accentuated by silvery folds that poked up from the neckline like space lace. "All I need is a blaster pistol and I could capture the spaceport for the alliance."

Flo and TC let their giggles escape. Agnes' lips curved upward in a slow grin.

"I think a helmet would be a nice touch," TC gasped out. "You could attach lace to the front instead of a visor."

They all burst out laughing, earning them the unwanted attention of the crabby sales lady. She'd been the source of the ugly dress, her tastes seemingly running toward the dreadful and bizarre. The fact that she was wearing her own spacesuit in shiny pink seemed proof of her questionable taste. "How are we doing, ladies?" he saleslady asked, her expression barely friendly.

"I think we need something less..." Ce fluttered her fingers on the air, searching in vain for the right word.

Agnes supplied it for her. "Ugly," she said, sending the other three into fits of laughter.

The sales woman's face puckered like she'd sucked a lemon. "I see. Well, we could go with something basic and black. I *had* assumed you wouldn't want to look like everyone else."

Agnes snorted. "I'd settle for looking like someone from this galaxy."

Sniffing her disgust at their pedestrian natures, the woman inclined her head. "I'll bring some more choices to the room."

The next outfit looked like something Willy Wonka would have rejected as an outfit for the Oompa-Loompas. It was a white tunic with giant pink polka dots, the sleeves voluminous and frothy and the hemline sewn with one-inch-wide golden rickrack.

"I haven't seen rickrack since I was seven years old," Celia said, clapping her hands in delight.

The pants that *matched* the tunic were hot pink and came to a spot midway down Agnes' calves, where it flared away from her leg, sporting more of the ugly gold rickrack.

Agnes cocked her head to the side and seemed to seriously be considering the garish outfit.

Flo thought she might puncture a lung, trying not to laugh.

"I'm just not sure what shoes I'd wear with this."

"I kind of like the puffy silver boots you tried on with the spacesuit," TC added helpfully.

"No," Ce said. "Black pumps will provide just the right statement."

"What statement is that?" Agnes asked with an arch of one eyebrow. "I'm a complete idiot?"

"Wait!" TC said, digging in her purse. She came out with a lipstick and hurried over to Agnes. "Hold still." She drew two perfect circles on Agnes' cheeks and smoothed them into pol-ka-dots that matched the dress. "There! That's perfect."

They burst into uncontrolled hilarity. Five minutes later, Agnes headed back to the dressing room, scrubbing at her cheeks with a tissue she'd gotten from Flo, and disappeared behind the curtain.

"This is better than a New York fashion show," Ce said, drying her tears of laughter.

"The outfits are about as weird," Flo agreed. "Maybe we should head to a shop that has more traditional, stuff."

"Where's the fun in that?" TC asked. She pulled a plastic jumpsuit off the rack and eyed it. "This is completely see-through," she exclaimed, alarmed.

"Wouldn't your handsome detective love that?" Ce asked, waggling her brows.

"I think you're supposed to wear those little stretchy bits underneath it," Flo said, pointing to the red bunches of elasticized cloth hanging over the hook affixed to the top of the hanger.

The sales lady hurried over and all but snatched the hanger from TC. "Customers never put things back the way they're supposed to be," she groused. She clipped a six-inch-wide stretchy band across the bottom of the hangar and shook it out. The second piece of stretchiness fell down beneath it, attached to the top by two threads on the sides.

"Those bottoms would barely cover my round booty," TC said, eyeing it with a doubt-filled expression.

"You have the perfect shape for this lovely piece," the woman said snootily. "In fact, you could wear any of this without a problem."

There was grudging approval in the woman's tone, and TC flushed with embarrassment. Flo figured that being told you could dress in any clownish costume and look good was hardly a compliment to her adorable younger friend.

"What do you guys think?"

They all turned to find Agnes standing just outside the dressing room, as if afraid to come any farther. She was wearing a softly draping black dress that hit her just at the knees. The square neckline and empire waist flattered her softly curved form, and the sheer sleeves with a slight flare at the hands were very feminine.

Agnes' expression was filled with genuine hope.

Celia clapped her hands. "You're gorgeous!"

TC grinned. "Agnes, that looks amazing on you."

Tears burned Flo's eyes. She felt like a mother seeing her teenaged daughter done up for her first prom. "You look so grown up."

Agnes' face lit up with happiness. "I love it too." She looked at the crabby sales lady. "I'll take this one."

The woman rolled her eyes and headed toward the front counter to await their approach with ill grace.

"She doesn't seem pleased with our choice. Maybe I should get the space boots to go with it," Agnes joked.

LE PETITE BISTRO WAS set back from Main Street in downtown Silver City. The entrance was a garden, with small wrought iron tables and chairs dotting the flagstone patio.

Enormous concrete planters overflowed with multi-colored faux mums, their sides draped with variegated ivy.

The door was black iron and glass, and slender trees in pots arched from either side to meet in the center of the glass transom window above the door.

The place was buzzing with activity, every visible table filled with smiling and chatting diners. Flo realized they probably should have called ahead with reservations. Though, at two o'clock in the afternoon, she'd never guessed the café would be busy.

They stood just inside the door, on large black and white tiles, gawking around at the quaint bistro and waiting for the busy hostess to seat them.

"Isn't this wonderful?" Celia said, her face alight with pleasure. "I'm getting all kinds of ideas for *Gioppino's*." She pointed to the ceiling, painted a matte black. "That's an elegant touch with the creamy orange walls."

Flo hoped Mass and Ce didn't change her favorite Italian restaurant too much. She kind of liked its dark, cozy atmosphere. Yes, it was a little worn in spots. But that was part of its homey charm.

"It's not very big," Agnes said with a frown. "I hope they can seat us."

Ce winked at Flo. "I think we'll be okay."

"CeCe, *mi amore*!"

A tall, dark-haired man hurried over, his handsome tanned face filled with pleasure as he swooped down on Celia. "I was so pleased to see you on the list." His accent was rich and rhythmic, pure French.

List? Flo and TC shared a look.

TC shrugged.

"François! Thanks for making room for my friends and me."

"Of course, beautiful lady. Of course." He swooped down on the podium, lifting a hand to the hostess to indicate he would take care of their party himself. The harried young woman nodded and headed toward a table in the back where she was being hailed. "My usual hostess isn't here tonight, so we're a bit off our game, I'm afraid."

"I hope she's all right?" Flo said, just making conversation.

"She's fine. I'm afraid her mother's sick, though."

They followed him through the room to a large round table in the back corner. It was covered in what looked like antique lace and featured a large basket of bread and croissants in its center. Two small black ceramic bowls holding soft, whipped butter sat alongside the basket.

François waited for them to take their seats and then handed the menus around. "Wine, CeCe?"

"Yes, please. Bring us a bottle of your best Pino Grigio," Ce told him.

He inclined his head. "On the house, of course." He stood back and smiled widely. "Enjoy your visit to Le Petite Bistro, ladies. And, please, let me know if I can do anything for you."

They watched him stride quickly away, his manner becoming animated as he spotted another group of diners at the door.

"Wow," TC said. "Is that the owner? How do you know him, Ce?"

"He's a friend of Mass' and mine. We've known him for years."

"How in the world did he end up in Silver City?" Flo asked.

"I don't know, really. Mass and I are always telling François and his lovely wife how much we love it here. They've had a restaurant in Indianapolis for several years. They still do. But I think François wanted to move out of the city. He wanted his kids to grow up in a small town."

"How old are the kids?" Agnes asked, grabbing a thick chunk of French bread from the basket.

"Twelve and fifteen. They're adorable."

A waiter arrived with their bottle of wine and everyone but Agnes waited until he'd left to hit the bread.

"I'm starving," TC said.

"Me too," Flo agreed. "That toast this morning didn't stay with me."

"Hey, isn't that the new guy over there? Pearce something?" Agnes eyed their new Silver Hills neighbor with interest.

Flo didn't miss Celia's grimace of distaste. "What is it, Ce? You ran off pretty fast when we bumped into Nicholai Pearce before. Do you know him?"

Ce's gaze skimmed sideways, but she nodded. "Mass has done business with the man. He's not a fan."

"What's wrong with him?" Agnes asked, breadcrumbs spraying the air around her.

Ce shrugged. "He's just not a nice man. He cheated on his wife, and when she was killed, he wasted no time trying to figure out how much money he could get his hands on from her death." She shook her head. "Mass hangs out with a lot of questionable characters, but though they straddle the legal line at times, I can't think of one who'd hurt a woman or a child. Aside from a malleable sense of legality, they're good men. Mass told me the first time he met Nic Pearce that the man was bad news. He did one deal with him, finding a buyer for a broach that had been in his wife's family for over a hundred years. Mass suspected Pearce's wife didn't know about the sale but he couldn't prove it and, unfortunately, the man came to him through one of Mass' best clients so he felt compelled to work with him. But he's never worked with him again."

"Was there any suspicion Pearce killed his wife?" Flo asked.

"Suspicion? Yes. Proof? No. Pearce is too slippery for that. If he killed that poor woman, he'd be sure to cover his tracks well."

Flo thought Ce was a little too hostile about Pearce to be judging him simply over a comment or two from her husband. She acted like a woman who'd been personally harmed by the man.

"Okay, fess up. What exactly does Mass do?" Agnes asked, reaching for a flaky croissant.

The table went very still, all eyes sliding to Agnes. She stopped mid-bite and frowned. "What? We all dance around this subject. It's stupid. Let's just get it out there and clear the air. Ce's our friend. We love her and Mass. Whatever she tells us will go into the vault."

Flo lifted a brow. "The vault, huh?"

Celia laughed, surprising them all. "And if somebody waves a cake or a pie in front of the vault, it won't spontaneously open and spew out everything it knows?"

Agnes chewed the buttery treat, glowering at Celia. She opened her mouth to respond, but Flo held up her hand. "Swallow first, please."

A beat later, Agnes put the croissant down on her plate. "I'm wounded that you think I would betray you and Mass for cake."

"Banana cream?" Ce asked, her brows lifting.

Agnes winced. "Are we talking a slice or the whole cake?"

"Agnes!" TC objected, laughing.

Agnes grinned. "Not even for a whole banana cream pie."

Ce sighed, growing serious. "You all know Mass doesn't like me to talk about his business."

Flo patted her hand. "We do, hun. And we understand. Don't give it a second thought."

Ce shook her head. "No. Agnes is right. I don't like keeping secrets from you. You're my best friends."

TC reached out and grasped Celia's hand. "We feel the same way about you."

Celia nodded. "The truth is, it's not as glamorous as what you think. Mass isn't a gangster. He's a fixer."

Flo felt her eyes go wide. "A fixer? What does that mean?"

"It means he has powerful connections on both sides of the law and sponsors who'll watch his back if he needs to step over a legal line or two. He takes big problems, messy ones, and finds solutions that protect his clients."

Agnes leaned over the table, her expression filled with interest. "He hides the bodies?"

Ce grimaced. "In a matter of speaking, yes."

"Sweet!" Agnes said, slapping the table beside her plate.

Everyone in the small restaurant stopped talking and looked her way.

Their waiter hurried toward them as if he thought she'd been signaling for him. "I'm so sorry to keep you waiting, ladies. Are we ready to order?"

Agnes grabbed her menu. "I don't know if you are," she told the man, "but I certainly am."

They gave the poor, frazzled waiter their orders. As soon as he hurried away, Agnes leaned across the table again. "Who's Mass' most important client?"

Ce paled. "I can't..."

"Well, look at all the beauties at this table," a too-smooth male voice said from behind Flo. She winced, recognizing the voice.

Half turning to look up at him, Flo gave him a neutral look. "Mr. Pearce. What a surprise."

He moved between her and Celia's chairs, his dark gaze lighting on TC. "Ms. Colombo. Just the young woman I wanted to see. I understand you offer yoga classes on Tuesday and Thursday afternoons."

TC's smile was genuine. "I do. Are you a yogi, Mr. Pearce?"

He threw back his head and laughed. "I bumble my way through. I find the bendiness of the moves so pleasant. Don't you?" He eyed TC carefully as he posed his question.

The oiliness of his innuendo permeated the entire table, staining their enjoyment of the outing. "Are you meeting someone, Mr. Pearce?" Flo asked, hoping to distract him from his unhealthy perusal of TC.

Pearce reluctantly swung his attention from their young friend, focusing on Flo. For just a beat, impatience or something darker, swept through his gaze. Then he smiled and it was gone. "I am. A business meeting." He glanced at his watch.

"And I'm going to be late if I don't get seated." He scanned the table, painting them with his easy smile. "It was a pleasure seeing you, ladies."

His gaze slithered over TC and he all but licked his lips. Then he strode quickly toward the front of the bistro, his hand outstretched as a young man in a nicely fitted suit took a seat near the windows. Two fierce-eyed men with square jaws and suspiciously bulging suit coats took up spots near the door as Pearce approached the table and shook Silver City's new, young mayor-elect's hand.

"What business do you suppose that snake has with Mayor-elect Potts," Ce mumbled.

"I don't know," Flo said, "But the sight of Pearce with that nice but very young man doesn't take me to my happy place."

"I wouldn't worry about Pearce having undue influence, Flo," TC said. "Dave Potts has his mother advising him and she's sharp as a tack."

TC wasn't wrong. Flo had met Nanna Potts and her son a couple of months earlier, when David Junior's father was killed in the middle of a fierce campaign to become mayor. He'd run against Silver Hills' own Vladwicke Newsome and, despite Vlad's extreme weirdness, had been barely ahead in the polls.

However, when Potts' personable son announced he was taking over his father's campaign, the sympathy vote took young David over the top and he handily beat Vlad.

Everything Flo had read and heard since then told her the young man and his advisor mother, a very politically astute woman in her own right, were working hard to create an administration that would be both effective and transparent.

Mayor-elect Potts' meeting with a man who was at worst shady and at best lacked good moral character was not a positive development.

"Whatever he wants, hopefully, young David will turn him down," Flo said.

The waiter arrived with their chicken crepes and fruit. They ate in companionable silence for a few minutes, commenting only on the deliciousness of the food.

Flo kept an eye on the Mayor and Pearce, noting the subtle clues that told her the conversation wasn't going well.

She was glad.

"Hey, there's Detective Peters," Agnes said, pointing her fork toward the door.

TC's head whipped around and she waved, catching the handsome young detective's eye. He smiled, heading quickly through the tables toward them.

"What are you doing here?" TC asked her boyfriend with a smile.

"Hey," Peters responded. He leaned down and kissed TC on the cheek. "I was coming to pick up a to-go order." He eyed the table. "Are those the chicken crepes?"

"Yes," Celia said. "And they're delicious."

"Good. That's what I ordered." He looked around the busy restaurant. "Nice place."

"Yes," Agnes said, waggling her shaggy brown eyebrows. "It's very romantic."

Peters gave her cop face. "I guess that means you and Hertz are spending date night here?"

Agnes turned bright red. "Actually, the engagement party is going to be here."

"Engagement? Did I miss an announcement?" Peters looked genuinely shocked.

Agnes' cheeks darkened to purple.

"No," Flo laughed. "Hertz Thomson's sister is getting married."

"How old is his sister?" TC asked with a frown.

"I think she's in her mid-forties," Agnes said on a shrug.

"Second marriage?" Ce asked.

"I don't think so. They're just marrying late."

Flo wondered if Hertz would marry late too, or if whatever it was that was making him jittery would keep him single for life. "Good for her," she said. "It doesn't hurt to be sure about someone before you marry them."

Peters and TC shared a look Flo couldn't decipher. She hoped it meant the two lovebirds were talking about nuptials. Flo couldn't wait to bounce a tiny TC on her knee. Realizing how far up the proverbial river she'd gone totally paddle-less, Flo tuned back into the conversation at the table.

"I'm working too. I figured I'd kill two birds with one stone," Detective Peters said.

Flo sat forward, lowering her voice. "You've got business at the Bistro? What exactly is it?"

Peters' expression went blank. "I can't tell you that. But you'll know soon enough." His gaze slid toward the Mayor's table, giving the young politician a speculative look.

A sense of horror filled her chest. "You're not going to arrest Mayor Potts..." she choked out.

Peters tore his gaze from the front table and arched a brow. "Your imagination is something else, Mrs. Bee. You should be writing mysteries along with Tricia."

TC shushed him, glancing quickly around. Her contract at Silver Hills did not allow for her to work a second job. And, while writing mysteries at home in her spare time didn't seem to be the kind of thing the management would object to, TC wasn't taking any chances. "Besides, I think Flo is better at investigating mysteries than she is at telling stories about them." TC sent Flo a fond look. "She can't sit still that long."

Flo laughed. "So true." But she wasn't about to be put off by the young detective's attempt at distraction. "Then what is it?" She had a thought and pulled a surprised gasp through her lips. "Has there been a threat on his life?"

Peters just shook his head as the hostess came out of the kitchen carrying a paper bag. "There's my lunch." He squeezed TC's shoulder. "I'll talk to you later?"

TC nodded enthusiastically.

As he paid for his food and left, Agnes eyed the big chalkboard on the wall facing the entrance. The day's specials were listed there. A main entrée, a special coffee, and a dessert. "They have blackberry cobbler!"

Flo tucked the last bite of crepe into her mouth, closing her eyes with pleasure.

"What about your diet?" TC asked softly.

Agnes had been working hard to get into better shape and be healthier. She'd done an excellent job too, having lost a considerable amount of weight and lowering her blood pressure to boot.

Flo was proud of her friend's accomplishment but understood that Agnes was not the type to give up things she loved forever. If she tried, she'd fail miserably and revert to her previous, unhealthy habits. "You could consider this your cheat meal for the week," Flo offered.

Agnes nodded. "I'm going to work out when we get home, and I won't eat dinner."

"Sounds perfect," Celia said, throwing TC a look.

TC was young and healthy and had no issues with wanting to eat too much. She just wasn't built that way. She was a kind person and truly wanted the best for her friends, but she had no idea of the real challenges in getting a bit older.

She'd find out soon enough.

In the meantime, she wasn't stupid. She knew when she was being set gently in her place. "Yes, that does sound perfect," she told Agnes with a smile. "I'd be up for a walk if you're all interested."

Celia patted her stomach, groaning softly. "I'd love a chance to work some of this off."

"Deal!" Flo said, grinning at TC.

Agnes grumblingly agreed. She hated walking. But she'd been doing more of it since she'd decided to get healthy.

With that happy thought in mind, the entire table ordered the cobbler. And then settled in with coffee and the decadent sweet, to revisit the high points of the afternoon's shopping event.

CHAPTER FOUR

Later that night, Flo was putting her teacup into the dishwasher when someone assaulted her door. Whoever it was sounded desperate, and that desperation infected Rodney. He was in the hallway, growling and barking with his tail straight up in the air, before Flo even reached the door.

"Who is it?"

"Open the door, doll!" Roger's voice sounded strained, tense.

"What's wrong?" she found herself asking even as she struggled with the deadbolt and wrenched it open.

To her vast surprise, he bolted inside, all but shoving her back as he pushed his way through, and earning himself a good barking from her startled dachshund for his troubles.

"What in the world? Roger, you nearly bowled me over."

The breach in polite behavior Roger was almost unerringly prone to shocked Flo, making her pulse pick up.

"I'm sorry, Flo." He hurried down the hallway into the living room and, wringing his hands together, he proceeded to pace back and forth in front of her couch. His lean, handsome face was gray and lined as if he'd aged ten years since she'd last seen him.

She hurried over and grabbed his arm, jerking him to a stop. "Roger Attles, you tell me what's wrong right this minute! You're scaring me."

He turned a haunted gaze downward, his eyes shiny with something that looked a lot like fear. "I...I might be in a lot of trouble," he told her.

"Trouble? Why..." the words fell away from her, unspoken as her gaze landed on his long-fingered hands.

To the fingertips that were coated in blood.

"Roger!" Flo exclaimed, pointing to the blood. "What happened? Are you hurt?"

He turned a pinched expression her way and shook his head. "I don't remember..." He scrubbed a hand over his face, smearing it with blood. "It's horrible." Roger took a step toward Flo and got a strange look on his face. He turned an unhealthy shade of gray and toppled sideways, hitting the couch and slamming his shoulder against the back.

"Roger!"

She hurried over to him as he rolled upright, his eyes fluttering open. Roger groaned, one hand coming up to test a spot on his head. There was blood there. But Flo wasn't sure if it was his or had been transferred from the blood on his hands.

She helped him sit upright again, propping pillows around him to keep him stable. "Roger, you need medical care. I'm going to call an ambulance."

His hand snaked out and clasped around her wrist, stopping her. "No. I need you to come..." he hesitated, swallowing hard and licking his lips. "...come with me to see."

"You're in no state to move, Roger."

He shook his head and pushed himself forward on the couch, weighting himself on his toes at the edge of it. "I just need a minute." He looked at his hands. "And I need to wash my hands, so I don't scare somebody in the halls."

She helped him into the bathroom and stood with a hand on his back as he liberally soaped up and spent several minutes rinsing his hands. Then he splashed cold water on his face and pronounced himself ready to go.

Flo stood nearby, wringing her hands. "You need to get to a doctor. Why don't we call Detective Peters and you can tell him where all that blood on your hands came from?"

Flo didn't want to admit it to herself, but she was worried about what Roger was going to show her. What if he'd hurt someone?

No. That wasn't possible. It was Roger. She'd never known a kinder, gentler man.

"Just do this for me, doll," he pleaded, his blue eyes bright with pain. "Please?"

She nodded. "Okay, let's get this over with so I can get you to the hospital." She grabbed her purse on the way out of the apartment, fully intending to coax him down to her car afterward and take him right to the emergency room.

Roger wobbled a bit on his feet as she locked her apartment, but he seemed to gain steam as they headed down the hallway. Flo kept her arm in his, just in case.

She realized after a moment that he was taking her to the singles side of the residence. She couldn't imagine what business he had there. Especially not business ending in bloodied hands. "Where are we going?"

"You've been there before, doll," Roger said evasively. He stumbled slightly, his face graying again as he raised a shaky hand toward his head.

"Roger Attles..."

He held out a hand to stop her. "Just a few more minutes. I promise."

She fumed silently, determined to make fast work of Roger's errand. The man looked ready to fall flat on his face. She briefly considered just dialing 9-1-1 and dealing with Roger's anger for it.

But then she realized where they were going. "Mae Caldone's place?"

He grunted softly. Apparently, that was all the response he could give her.

Flo eyed the pinched aspect of his face and the unhealthy sheen of sweat across his brow.

They reached the door and Flo realized it was ajar. It didn't look like it had been broken into. It was simply open.

She saw with a grimace that there was a large, bloody handprint on the flat surface, and more blood wrapped around the handle. Roger had clearly been there.

A terrible feeling made Flo's stomach churn. "Where did all the blood come from, Roger?"

He shoved the door open and stumbled inside, smacking up against a short wall that separated the rest of the apartment from the entrance and knocking a pretty, glass figurine of a dancer onto the floor on the other side.

He leaned against the wall, panting. "I just need to sit..." Roger slid down the wall, resting his head against it and sighing wearily. "I'll be good as new in a minu..." Roger's eyes rolled back in his head and his chin hit his chest.

"Roger!" Flo hurried over and checked his pulse, finding it fast but strong. She quickly examined his head and saw a large goose egg there. No wonder he was so unsteady. He probably had a concussion.

She dialed 9-1-1 and told them where she was. Then she stood up and looked into Mae Caldone's apartment over the short wall.

The kitchen was a wreck. Broken glass littered the floor. The walls were missing large chunks of drywall as if someone had thrown something heavy and-or sharp at them. Flo moved slowly inside, realizing the glass was from Roger's mother's tea set.

All those beautiful antiques...the faded pink roses blooming over creamy yellow porcelain...destroyed.

What in the world had happened in there? Was that how Roger had gotten so bloody? Had he cut himself on the broken dishes? No. There'd been no cuts on his hands when he'd washed them.

Then had Mae cut herself? Had he been helping her? Flo forced herself to step deeper into the apartment. She moved carefully around the island in the small kitchen and into the tiny living space. The mess seemed to be mostly contained to the kitchen. Only a couple of small tables and one chair were turned over in the main living space.

Blood stained the back of Mae's small couch, vibrant against the cabbage rose on white print of the delicate furniture.

It took Flo only a second to find the source of the blood.

Mae was crumpled in one corner, looking like a broken rag doll. Her throat had been sliced from ear to ear by a large shard of porcelain, which rested against her shoulder on the blood-saturated white carpet as if the killer had just dropped it there.

Flo's heart beat hard against her ribs. She quickly looked around, seeing no evidence that the killer was still in that room. Fighting the urge to turn and run, she pulled a tissue from a box on the table and used it to open the few doors in the place.

No heartless killer lurked in the two closets. There were no murderers hiding in the single, small bath.

She was alone in the apartment except for Roger.

And the woman whom everybody was going to believe he'd killed.

FLO WATCHED THE AMBULANCE roll away into the night, her stomach in knots with worry about Roger. She was torn between two conflicting desires. She needed to go to the hospital to make sure Roger was going to be okay. And she needed to stay at Silver Hills and figure out what happened to that poor young woman.

Footsteps came up behind her as she stood there, suddenly too weary to decide which imperative was more pressing.

A hand found her shoulder. She turned to look into Richard Attles worried face. "I'm going to go sit with him. He wants you to stay here and find out what's going on."

Tears burned in her eyes. "He spoke to you?"

Roger hadn't been coherent enough when the EMTs arrived in Mae Caldone's apartment to tell her or Detective Peters what happened. And she'd been detained with what felt like a thousand questions from the detective before she could come down and see him.

By the time she ran out the door, the ambulance was just pulling out of the Silver Hills lot, lights flaring into the night.

Richard nodded. "He told me he was fine. Just had a headache. And that you needed to find out what happened to Mae."

Flo wrapped her arms around herself. "Did you speak to the EMTs?"

"I did. They backed up what he said. His vitals are strong. There's no sign of any internal distress. No broken bones. He has a knot on his head and a lot of pain." Richard squeezed her arm. "I'll go sit with him tonight. You can come tomorrow if you want."

Flo nodded. "Thank you, hun. Tell him I'll be there in the morning, okay?"

"You got it." He started to walk away and stopped, turning back. He seemed to be considering his words for a long moment, his expression filled with worry.

"What is it, Richard?"

"He needs your help, Flo. Nobody else will look past the circumstantial evidence and dig for the truth."

Flo realized what Richard was telling her. He'd seen the bloody handprint on the door. He'd noticed the family antiques shattered all over the floor. He knew.

Roger was in deep trouble.

And he was right. Flo knew in her heart that she was Roger's best hope to be cleared. Detective Peters was a good cop. But he prided himself on not allowing personal feelings to get in the way of his police work. He'd look at the evidence in a cold, clinical way and come to the simplest conclusion. It was true that, most times, the simplest explanation was the right one. But in this case, Flo knew that tried and true formula would lead to an innocent man being accused of Mae Caldone's murder.

And she wasn't going to let that happen.

CHAPTER FIVE

Officer Nicholas Bachus waved to Flo as she hurried toward Mae's apartment. His brown eyes widened slightly when he saw the determined set to her face and realized she was going to stride right past him.

Throwing out an arm, Bachus cut her off before she could dodge around him and duck inside. "Whoa there, Mrs. Bee. Where do you think you're going?"

The faint scent of stale tobacco wafted off the young officer, telling her he hadn't quit smoking yet. Flo pointed toward the open door, which was currently undergoing fingerprint dusting by Officer Meldick. "Detective Peters wanted to speak to me." Flo felt a tiny bit bad about deceiving the young officer, who was young enough to respect his elders but not yet old enough to understand how devious they could be.

Unfortunately for Flo, Bachus seemed to have gotten a bit wiser since the last time she'd met up with him on the wrong side of an investigation. "Sorry, Mrs. Bee. He's processing the scene. You'll have to wait out here."

Flo huffed, fixing the twenty-something cop with her best school teacher look. "I have important information for the detective. You don't want to be the one who keeps me from getting it to him, do you?"

"Nice try, Mrs. Bee," an oily voice drawled.

She looked up to see Officer Jason Meldick, dubbed Meanie Meldick by Flo and Co, lumbering her way. He dragged his six hundred pounds across the ten yards between them, wearing a mean smile on his round face.

A hairy guy at the best of times, Meldick's lumpy cheeks were sporting the beginnings of a beard by that time of night. "Don't believe anything this one says," he told Bachus. "She's as slippery as an eel."

Flo bit back a rebuttal, mostly because he was right. She and her friends had cajoled, tricked, and downright lied to Meldick in the past, going so far as to use poor Agnes, whom he seemed to have a crush on, to distract him while they performed their "on the edge of legal" shenanigans behind his back. "Officer Meldick. How are you this evening?"

His response was a snort. "I'm not falling for any of your tricks tonight, Mrs. Bee, so you can save them." He jerked his massive head toward the seating area nearby. "Have a seat there. If he feels like it, Detective Peters will talk to you when he's done processing the scene."

Irritation flared and Flo barely kept from poking him in his meaty chest. But she held onto her dignity by the thinnest of threads. "If you'd be so kind as to tell him I'd like to speak with him, I'd be very grateful."

Meldick snorted again and headed back to his fingerprint dusting.

Flo looked at Bachus. He twitched under her glare and nodded. "I'll go tell him. You promise you'll wait out here?"

Flo promised and meant it. She had no desire to get the young officer in trouble. Though if Peters didn't come out of that apartment soon, she wasn't sure what she was going to do. She couldn't shake the feeling that every moment Peters was in there alone, gathering his own suspicions, was a moment of opportunity lost in Roger's defense.

She tried to sit down but couldn't stay still. So she got up and started to pace.

Five minutes later, Peters came out of the apartment, pulling a pair of latex gloves off his hands as he glanced up and spotted her. He looked tired as he strolled over to her, his broad shoulders drooping. "Mrs. Bee. Did you really have information for me? Or is this just a ploy to find out what's going on."

She thought about the question for a moment and then decided to be honest. "Both. My information is that Roger was hit over the head and doesn't recall what happened. Unless you believe he killed that poor woman and then hit himself over the head, you can't seriously be considering him a suspect in Mae Caldone's murder."

Peters lifted his brows. "I can't?"

Flo twisted her hands together and fought the urge to snap at him. "Look, Detective Peters, Roger couldn't have killed that poor woman. He has no motive. He barely knew her. And if you know Roger at all, you know he just isn't capable of that type of thing."

"Mrs. Bee, I understand you have feelings for Mr. Attles..."

"My feelings have nothing to do with this."

"Of course they do," Peters said, gently. "You love the man. It's hard for you to see him as being capable of doing anything bad."

"I knew it." she nearly shouted. "I figured you'd take the simplest path and blame him, just because it's easier."

Peters' square jaw tightened. Anger lit his intense hazel gaze. "Are you accusing me of doing shoddy police work?"

Flo took a deep breath. "I'm sorry. I didn't mean to impugn your motives."

"Yes, I believe you did," he growled out.

She bit back irritation and inclined her head. "You're right. I'm angry and scared, and I'm taking it out on you. Can we start over?"

He nodded. "I'll start. It might surprise you to learn that I'm not convinced Roger Attles killed Mae Caldone."

Relief flooded her. It must have shown in her face because he held up a hand in caution. "Don't assume that means I've removed him from the list of possible suspects because I haven't. Even you have to admit it looks bad."

She did have to admit that. If only to herself. It was why she was so terrified. "You aren't going to find a motive, Detective. Roger never met that woman before and he barely knew her."

"That doesn't mean he didn't kill her. Eleven percent of homicides are committed by strangers. To muddy the waters even more, the non-stranger designation includes even casual acquaintance. Do you really believe that, when I start digging into this, I'll find out that Roger Attles and Mae Caldone had zero interaction? They both live under the same roof, Mrs. Bee. They're both single adults...I'm sorry if that offends you but it's true...and Mr. Attles himself admitted they were transacting the sale of some antiques."

Tears burned Flo's eyes. She angrily blinked them back. "He didn't kill her."

Peters stared down at her for a beat, his expression neutral, unreadable. Then he softened, taking her arm and walking her farther down the hall. "I'm sorry this is causing you pain, Flo. You might not believe it, but I don't want to hurt you or Mr. Attles if he's innocent. I have a job to do. Evidence to gather. Having you in my face, fighting the process the entire way, isn't going to help Roger."

"I know," she said, working to calm the racing of her heart. "But I won't stand down from this, Detective. I won't pretend that I'm going to sit back while the evidence points a finger at an innocent man."

"Thank you for your honesty. I figured as much. Which is why I'm going to make a deal with you. As long as you don't obstruct my investigation, I'll look the other way as you do what you need to do. But you have to keep me apprised of anything you discover. Deal?"

It was more than fair. But Flo couldn't help trying to get more from him. "I'll agree to those terms if you'll agree to share what you discover with me too."

"You know I can't do that."

She pressed her lips together, anger making her breathing tight. She was afraid to speak for fear she'd say something they both regretted. So she stiffly inclined her head and turned on her heel, striding quickly down the hall toward the main stairs as the Detective called her name behind her.

She'd play it by ear, sharing only what she thought might help Roger or earn her information in return. But if Detective Peters wasn't going to reciprocate with information, Flo wasn't going to give him anything that might help him make a case against Roger.

And if that made him mad, so be it. The man was as stubborn as a mule. And he could just go pound sand as far as she was concerned.

AGNES RAN UP TO FLO as she headed toward the small bar area to the side of the dining room. She was going to start talking to residents to find out if anybody knew who might have wanted to hurt Mae.

"Flo! I just heard. Is Roger all right?"

Flo scrubbed a hand over her eyes, her stress level rocketing upward. She'd forgotten to check on Roger. She needed to call Richard and see how his father was doing. "I don't know. I think so. I've been talking to Mr. Rockhead upstairs and haven't had a chance to speak to Richard."

Hertz came up to them, his pleasant face filled with concern. "Is it true, Flo? Was somebody murdered?"

Flo nodded. "A woman over on the singles side. Mae Caldone. Did you know her?"

Hertz shook his head, his gaze sliding to Agnes and then shifting quickly away. "I don't believe we've met. What did she look like?"

Flo described her as Elisa Kemp scurried over, her long, too-thin frame bent like a praying mantis and her dark eyes filled with excitement. "Mae's really dead? Oh my goodness. Do the police have a suspect?"

Flo shook her head. She refused to put Roger's reputation on the chopping block. "Not yet. Roger was injured too."

"Roger?" Elisa feigned surprise, but Flo realized the other woman had probably already heard and promptly spread the rumors about Roger and the attractive younger single. Her lips compressed into a firm line as irritation flared. But she wouldn't let pique derail her. Elisa Kemp could help Flo find Mae's killer and remove Roger from the list of suspects. "Elisa, I need you to talk to everybody who knew Mae. I need to know if she'd been scared lately, or if she'd been acting strangely. If she'd mentioned anybody who might want to hurt her."

Elisa nodded, mentally filing each question away.

Flo thanked the other woman and watched her march back toward the bar. She felt confident Elisa would ferret out anyone with any information at Silver Hills.

Agnes moved closer, lowering her voice. "Flo, what was Roger doing at that woman's place tonight?"

By the way Agnes asked, Flo realized her friend suspected Roger of being unfaithful. She shook her head. "It's not what you're thinking, Agnes. He was selling her some of the stuff from storage downstairs. He must have walked in on something. It's the only thing that makes sense."

Agnes and Hertz shared a look. Flo didn't miss it. "What? Tell me."

Hertz's eyes widened and Agnes sighed. "People were talking about this woman in the bar a minute ago, Flo. She apparently had quite a reputation."

"Reputation? For what?"

Agnes' cheeks pinkened.

"Oh. Well, those kinds of rumors are usually just jealousy speaking. Mae Caldone was a very nice woman."

"I'm sure she was, Flo," Hertz said. "But she's dated a good portion of the men in this residence. Word was she'd already taken up with that new guy."

Flo nodded. "Nicholai Pearce. Mae told me about him. He was being very aggressive with her. He's next on my list of people to talk to."

"You can't talk to that guy alone, Flo," Agnes said, shaking her head. "He might be dangerous. If he's threatened Mae and now she's dead, that makes him the prime suspect."

"I agree. I was hoping to get Mass to go with me."

"Mass?" Hertz asked, looking confused.

"Celia's husband," Agnes clarified. "Have you spoken to Ce?"

"Not yet. I'm going to do that next."

"Okay, I'll come with you," Agnes said.

"I don't think that's a good idea, Agnes," Hertz said, frowning. "Massimo Angonetti is a mobster. He's dangerous."

Agnes blew a raspberry. "Mass is a friend. He'd never hurt one of us."

Hertz didn't look convinced. He also didn't look happy with how Agnes blew his opinion off. But Flo couldn't worry about Hertz's feelings right in that moment. The two of them would have to work that out on their own.

"I'm going to go grab Rodney and my purse. I'll meet you at Ce's in a few minutes?"

"See you there," Agnes agreed.

As Flo hurried away, she heard Hertz and Agnes arguing in a subdued tone. She almost smiled. If Hertz thought he was going to change Agnes' mind about anything once she'd made it up, maybe he wasn't the man for her friend after all. He should have known her better than that.

She dialed Richard Attles' phone on the way upstairs. Richard answered on the second ring. "Hi, Flo."

"Richard. How is he?"

"He's fine. He's had some pain meds and he's settled in a room. He's already cracking jokes with the nurses. You can stop worrying about him for tonight and get some rest. He says he's looking forward to seeing you *tomorrow*. The emphasis was his, not mine."

Flo would not stop worrying about him. Not for a minute. But it was okay if Richard and Roger didn't know that. "Oh, that is good news. I'll leave him in your very capable hands. Thanks so much, Richard."

Flo felt a tiny bit guilty for not asking to speak to Roger, but she needed to keep her head in the game. Next, she dialed up Celia. Her friend answered after three rings, her voice breathless. "Hello?"

"Did I catch you at a bad time?"

"Hey, Flo! No, I was just washing my face and had to run to catch you before it rolled to voicemail. What's up? Are you okay?"

"Not really. Can Agnes and I come up in a few minutes? I have something I need to talk to you about."

"Sure. I'll make some tea. See you in a few."

CHAPTER SIX

Celia looked ten years younger when she answered her door. She wore no makeup and had her hair pulled back in a stretchy headband like the ones Flo used to wear when she was in school. Despite a few telltale wrinkles around the eyes and mouth, Celia Angonetti was a very well-preserved woman in her late fifties. "What a nice surprise!" She reached out and clasped Flo's hand, tugging her inside. "Hey, Agnes, I have a nice surprise for you," Celia told Agnes.

"What kind of surprise?" Agnes asked in a suspicious tone.

"Cook made another one of her sugar-free pies and I got us three slices."

Flo was shocked. "Cook was still in the kitchen at this hour?"

"She likes to get ahead of her baking after hours. She says its soothing to be in there with nobody getting in her way."

"I can certainly understand that," Flo said.

Celia nodded. "She sent Natasha up with the slices. Did you pass her on the stairs?"

"No. She must have gone down the back stairwell," Flo said. "I'm surprised to hear Natasha was here this late too."

Natasha Sabitov was the sister of a man who'd worked in the kitchen until his death. When he'd been killed, Natasha had taken her brother's job and worked her way up to being one of Cook's most trusted assistants.

"I don't think Cook does anything without Natasha anymore. I get the feeling she's grooming her to take over as chef if Cook ever leaves us."

"Bite your tongue," Agnes said. "Cook's not allowed to leave."

"I hear ya." Ce led them into her bright kitchen and pointed toward the table. "Sit. Would you like ice cream with your pie?" Celia asked Agnes.

"Does the Pope poop in the woods?" Agnes answered.

That made Ce frown thoughtfully. "Gosh, I hope not. That would be undignified."

Agnes shrugged. "Campers do it all the time."

"I knew there was a reason or fifteen why I never wanted to go camping," Flo said.

Celia handed them tea and set about fixing their plates of pie. "So tell me what's going on. You look worried, Flo."

"I am worried. Very worried." She filled Ce in on Mae Caldone's murder and Roger's inadvertent involvement.

Celia listened carefully without speaking until Flo was done. She settled forks and napkins on the table next to the plates and sat down with them. "Poor Roger."

Flo nodded. "The worst part is that Detective Peters is gearing up to blame Roger for the murder."

"He's a good cop, Flo," Celia said, sipping her tea. "He's not going to pin anything on Roger the evidence doesn't implicate him on. And there's not going to be any evidence that Roger killed that woman because he didn't kill her." Celia lowered a finger covered in ice cream for Rodney to lick.

"I agree," Flo said, wishing that made her feel better. "But I'm going to run my own investigation anyway, just to make sure all the facts are brought out into the open."

Celia nodded. "What can I do to help?"

"I want Mass' help with Nicholai Pearce."

Celia blinked for a moment, clearly shocked. "You think Nic Pearce is involved in this?"

"I do. I saw him in a very heated argument with Ms. Caldone on the street just yesterday. Mae later told me that he's been aggressively possessive of her, and she'd broken it off. I'm thinking a man like Nic Pearce wouldn't like being punted to the curb very much."

"No, he certainly would not," Celia agreed. "I'm glad you came to me. I'm assuming you want Mass to talk to Nic?"

"Not quite. I'm going to talk to him myself. I just wanted to borrow some muscle for protection when I do."

MASSIMO ANGONETTI WAS many things, but subtle wasn't one of them.

Flo stood under the early winter night sky and shivered. Flo's body was having trouble keeping up with the manic changes in weather. The day had started out wet, and the temps had dropped a good twenty degrees by the time Agnes and Flo made it to *Riverdale Cemetery*. She tugged her coat closer, wishing she'd worn a heavier one for their outing. Though, in her defense, when she'd prepared to leave, she hadn't known Mass' chosen meeting spot would be outdoors.

Inside her car, Rodney barked incessantly, irritated as only a dachshund could be about being left behind. But Flo didn't trust him not to poop on a gravestone or something.

Agnes stood next to her, wearing a sweatshirt and a pair of jeans. She'd pulled a sleeveless, down vest on at the last minute, but she wasn't wearing a hat or gloves. And, as a chilly breeze slashed through the gravestones, slicing like razors across her exposed skin, Flo wondered at Agnes' capacity to create her own heat.

"Are you sure this is the right place?" Agnes asked again. Her friend had asked the question several times, her wide face filled with doubt as she looked around the empty cemetery. "We seem to be the only ones here."

Flo was getting a little worried about that. Had Mass meant to send them somewhere else and just gotten mixed up? She'd thought meeting in a cemetery was maudlin at best and downright aggressive at worst. Though the symbolism behind it made Flo grin.

Mass had a reputation of being a gangster and he took great pleasure in playing the "swim wit da fishes" metaphor to its max.

A big, black car entered the cemetery and began to wind its way slowly toward Flo and Agnes.

The volume of Rodney's barking increased and he threw his little body against the driver's side door.

"Here's Mass," Flo told her friend. "Ce told me they'd be in a black Lincoln Town car."

The big car glided to a stop behind Flo's sedan and sat for a long moment before a back door opened and a tall man with thick, graying dark-brown hair stepped out and slid an assessing golden-brown glance over them.

He smiled. "Ladies."

Massimo Angonetti was ruggedly handsome, with a piercing gaze and a square jaw that always seemed in need of a shave.

Agnes gave Mass a little finger wave, and Flo stepped forward to shake his hand. "Thank you so much for doing this, Mass. I'm sorry to intrude on your day."

He shook his head, turning slightly as the driver's side door opened. A mountain of muscles with small, dark-brown eyes stepped out.

Rodney growled at the big man. Mass' bodyguard growled back, causing Rodney to cock his head and whine.

Mass returned his gaze to Flo, squeezing her hand before dropping it. "It's no problem at all. You know I'm happy to help you any time."

She inclined her head. "Much appreciated."

Mass' muscle crossed massive arms over his chest as he sat back against the car door. Vincent Sarbono nodded a greeting but stayed next to the car, his gaze sliding toward the cemetery entrance.

Flo wasn't surprised Mass had brought his bodyguard. Mass didn't really do much without Vincent. "Obviously Pearce isn't here yet. What can you tell me about him? What should I know?"

"He's a snake and a reprobate. Don't trust anything he says and definitely don't let him get too close. He has no scruples at all when it comes to women."

Flo's eyes widened. "You think he's capable of sexual assault?"

"And then some. I've asked Ce to keep her distance from him." He frowned. "In fact, now that the man's living at Silver Hills, I'm trying to talk her into moving."

"Oh no!"

Mass nodded, giving her an apologetic smile. "I'm sorry, Flo. But her safety is my number one concern at all times." At Flo's crestfallen look, Mass added, "She wouldn't be far away. You could still be friends."

Flo fought a sense of foreboding. It seemed like everybody was leaving Silver Hills all of the sudden. "I understand you want to keep her safe. Has he..." Flo hesitated, not sure if she was approaching a subject she had no business addressing. But Mass wasn't shy. If she was overstepping he'd let her know. "Did he do something to Ce?"

Mass' frown deepened. "He would have if Vincent hadn't arrived in time. It was about twenty years ago. Pearce might not even remember her. He was a total tomcat in those days. Old age has slowed him down some." Mass' smile held no humor. "He's lucky Vincent was the one who found him trying to force a kiss on her and not me. If it had been me, his body would have never been found."

After what Celia had told them about Mass' occupation, Flo believed him. "His obsession with women seems to be pretty common knowledge," Flo said. "Do you believe he's capable of murder?"

She expected Mass to deny it but he hesitated, seeming to consider the possibility. Finally, he inclined his head. "Under the right circumstances. I don't know if romantic rejection would be enough of a trigger though. He's had a lot of experience with that."

"You're saying that, if he killed Mae Caldone, it would have been for another reason? Like maybe she knew something about him he didn't want getting out?"

"That seems the most likely scenario, yes."

A red, two-door sports car turned into the cemetery. Flo shook her head at the obviousness of Pearce's choice in cars. Pearce was a walking cliché of a man undergoing a middle-age crisis.

Pearce stopped the sportscar in the middle of the cemetery road and climbed out. Flo was certain it never occurred to the man that he might be blocking someone from getting past. His brain seemed to be stuck in permanent "me, myself, and I" mode.

Rodney's growls turned vicious as he flung himself against the glass, teeth bared. The little dog didn't like the looks of Nicholai Pearce at all.

Pearce skimmed Vincent a look, his expression tightening, and then strolled toward the rest of them with slightly aggressive strides.

He nodded at Mass. "Angonetti. I was surprised to get your call."

"This is Mrs. Bee's show. I'm just here for moral support."

Pearce snorted out a laugh. "Moral support, huh? She really dragged the bottom of the barrel for that one."

Vincent pushed off the car, his hands fisting as he glowered in Pearce's direction.

Mass held out a hand, signaling for Vincent to stand down. "You aren't exactly known for respectful treatment of the ladies. Mrs. Bee is a personal friend of mine. I'd be very upset if anything happened to her."

Pearce shook his head, a grim smile on his lips. "Message received. I have no intention of harming this woman." He slid a sneer over her. "She's not my type."

Flo bristled at the insult. He was implying she was too old. The dig hurt. But she quickly reminded herself why they were there. "Mr. Pearce, I wanted to ask you about Mae Caldone."

Surprise lit his handsome face. "Mae? What about her?"

"What do you know about her murder?"

His brows lifted in what appeared to be genuine surprise. "Mae was murdered?" He stumbled back a couple of steps, and Flo watched with a mix of surprise and doubt. Either Pearce really hadn't known Mae was dead, or he was a very good actor.

Flo wasn't ready to give up on the idea that he was acting a part. "Are you telling me you didn't know?"

Pearce ran a hand over his face, his mouth falling open as he shook his head. "I've been in Indianapolis for a couple of nights. I just got back."

"What were you doing in Indy?" Flo asked.

His expression sharpened. "That's none of your business."

She nodded. "I'm sure Detective Peters will ask. I'll just get the information from him."

Pearce laughed. "You expect me to believe the cops will share information about a murder investigation with you?" His lips twisted with disdain.

She forced herself to remain calm. He was baiting her, expecting her to become emotional. Pearce had dealt with a lot of women, but he clearly had no respect for the gender. "You can believe it or not. I don't much care, Mr. Pearce. I often work with the police on cases. Detective Peters asked me to run a parallel investigation since Mae was a friend."

Okay, that was a stretch of the truth, but Flo kept a straight face as she delivered it.

"So he's using nosy old ladies as PIs these days?" He barked out a laugh.

Flo reached into her purse and pulled out one of the business cards she'd recently had made. It had taken several months working with the State, but she'd also registered an LLC for her new investigative agency. "Busy Bee Private Investigations," she said as she handed it to him. "Whatever your problem, we'll Bee there." She barely kept from smiling as she gave them her new tagline.

Pearce scanned a look at the card and then shoved it into his shirt pocket. He shook his head. "I wasn't aware you and Mae even knew each other." He narrowed his eyes. "You think I killed her." It wasn't a question. It was a realization.

Flo held his stare.

"Why would I do that?"

"I don't know, Mr. Pearce. That's why I'm asking. Mae seemed to think she needed to file a restraining order against you. She said you were stalking her."

Pearce laughed. "The woman was delusional." He stared down at the ground for a while and then glanced back up at her. "I'll tell you where I was because I don't want you to keep pestering me. I was with a lady friend in Indianapolis. We went to the Indianapolis Museum of Art and then to the Pied Piper Restaurant on Meridian. You can check both of those out, and you'll learn I'm telling the truth."

Flo nodded. "And the woman's name?"

Pearce seemed to be considering the question. For a moment, Flo thought he might actually tell her. She could probably get the woman's name if she followed Pearce's trail to Indianapolis, but she'd rather not take the time to do that if she could avoid it. She was cognizant of the ticking clock nature of the investigation. It would take Detective Peters a lot less time to dig up the information, but there was no guarantee he'd share it with her.

"No. I'm sorry, Mrs. Bee. That's really none of your business." He glanced at Mass, then Vincent before giving her a jaunty wave. "I'll see you around."

Flo watched him climb into his car and drive away, a sinking feeling in her chest.

"You want me to have somebody beat the information out of him?" Mass asked with a straight face.

Vincent enthusiastically cracked his knuckles, looking more than up for the job.

Mass' voice startled her and she turned. "No. But thanks for the offer. I'll keep it in mind."

He grinned, knowing she wouldn't, but enjoying that she'd played along. "If you need anything else, don't hesitate to call."

"I won't. Thanks, Mass."

"I mean it, Flo. That guy's dangerous. Don't take any chances with him."

"I won't."

Mass squeezed her shoulder and headed back to the Town car. It wasn't until the big car pulled away from the curb that Flo remembered Agnes. She turned on her heel, shocked that her usually cocky friend hadn't spoken a word during the whole interchange.

She found Agnes standing several feet away, her gaze following Pearce's too-fast exit from the cemetery. "You were awfully quiet," she told her friend.

Agnes dragged her gaze from the little red car. "That guy gives me the creeps." She put her head down and moved quickly toward Flo's car, sliding into the passenger seat without further comment.

Flo frowned. Something wasn't right there. Agnes was hiding something from her. And Flo couldn't leave it be. With Roger's freedom on the line, there would be no secrets left uncovered at Silver Hills.

CHAPTER SEVEN

"I told you nothing's wrong," Agnes insisted as they pushed through the front doors into Silver Hills the next morning. Flo had taken Agnes out for breakfast in the hopes she could get her to open up about Hertz, Pearce, and anything else that was bothering her.

"You promise you'd tell me if there was?" Flo asked.

"I promise." Agnes sounded sincere, but her gaze kept sliding away from Flo. She still wasn't convinced.

"There you are!" Elisa Kemp said, scurrying toward them as they crossed the lobby. "I have news on our case."

Flo didn't miss the "our" and bit back the urge to clarify. She guessed, in a way, she'd recruited Elisa on the case. Every good investigator needed ears on the ground. Elisa Kemp served that role well. "What is it?"

"I've been checking around and found a few people you should definitely talk to." She pulled out a small pad of paper. "Renee Woldigger heard Mae arguing with some man in the workout room. Renee's pretty sure she's seen the man there before. It might be somebody who lives here."

"Did she give you a description of the guy?"

"Not a good one. She said late forties, early fifties, graying hair. Attractive." Elisa made a face. "Keep in mind, Renee is a spinster of a certain age and she pretty much thinks every man is attractive. She also has no idea about age. She thought Old Mrs. Peabody was in her fifties."

Flo grimaced. Old Mrs. Peabody was ninety-three if she was a day. "Okay, thanks, Elisa."

Elisa held up a long, spidery finger. "There's more. Cook saw Pearce arguing pretty aggressively with a petite blonde woman at the market a few days ago."

"She's sure the woman was blonde? Not a redhead?"

"I asked her that question and she said the woman's hair was almost white. A very distinctive color."

Flo doubted that was Mae, but she needed to check it out anyway. "Okay, I'll talk to Cook. Anything else?"

"Not yet. I'm still digging."

"There's one avenue you might want to explore." Flo told her about Pearce's museum date. "It's a long shot, but maybe the woman who is apparently his alibi lives in Silver City. If he's encouraging her to lie for him, we might be able to determine that if we talk to her."

Eliza jotted it down. "Any physical attributes for the woman?"

"No. Sorry. I was lucky to get what I did from him."

"Okay, I'll see what I can find."

"Thanks, Elisa. I'll buy you dinner when this is all over."

She lifted her pen, smiling. "I'll take you up on that. Even though this is more fun than I've had in ages."

Flo turned to Agnes, who was still suspiciously quiet behind her. "Let's go."

Agnes fell into step beside her, hurrying to keep up. "Where are we going?"

"To Mae Caldone's apartment. I'm hoping we can get inside. Mass' suggestion that she might have had something against Pearce intrigues me."

"You think Detective Peters would have missed something like that?"

"Not likely. But there's always a chance."

Flo passed through the center hallway that went from the singles side to the senior side on the first floor. The section connected the two-story annex at the back of the building that represented the single side.

Common services, such as the mailroom, cash machines, and a concierge window were also located in the center hallway. Despite that, it was mostly only used by people on the singles side who lived on the first floor.

Flo used it because it was a less conspicuous approach.

"How are we going to get past the cop at the door," Agnes asked. She was no doubt worrying that it would be Meldick and she'd be called on to fake flirt with him again.

"I'm not sure. I'm winging it here."

A short, balding man wearing a postman's uniform and heavy black glasses that all but took over his small face came out of the mailroom with a handful of mail. He was frowning.

"Hi, Bill," Agnes said, giving him a smile and a wave.

"Oh, hey, Agnes. Flo."

"How are you?" Flo asked, intending to walk on by.

"I've been better."

"What's wrong?" Flo felt obligated to stop since she'd asked. Though she'd meant it as a rhetorical question.

"I tried to deliver this mail to Mae Caldone, but there's a sticker on her box that says to give any incoming mail to the police." He sighed. "I don't have time to make a side trip today." Shaking his head, he almost dislodged the oversized glasses. Shoving them up his nose with a stubby finger, Bill the Mailman offered them a weary smile. "I'd best get going. See you later."

Inspiration struck Flo. "We can deliver that to the police if you'd like. We're heading to her apartment now, and there's a uniformed officer there."

Bill seemed unsure. "I shouldn't give it to you. It's addressed to her."

Just Flo's luck Bill would be a stickler for the rules. "I understand. It was just a thought."

"You could come up with us," Agnes said. "And give the mail to him yourself."

Bill scowled at his watch and then looked at the mail. Finally, he sighed. "You wouldn't mind just handing it over to the police for me?"

"Not at all," Flo said, holding out her hand for the envelopes.

"That would be wonderful." Bill tugged his too-tight blue shirt. "I promised the wife I'd do some Christmas shopping with her this afternoon." He grimaced. "I can't believe Christmas is only a few weeks away," he groused. "She's frantic to get everything done early so she can, and I quote, 'Enjoy the season.'"

"I totally understand," Flo said, her hand still outstretched.

Despite his obvious reluctance, Bill placed the short stack of mail into her hand. "Thanks again. I'll drop into the precinct in the morning to make sure they got it."

It was said off-handedly, but the implied threat was there.

"Don't worry," she assured him. "Mail theft is a federal offense. I don't need that kind of trouble."

He had the good grace to look sheepish. "Well. I'd best get going."

"What's the plan?" Agnes asked, hurrying after Flo as she moved quickly toward the smaller lobby of the singles side.

"If there's a cop at the door, we'll give him this and tell him there might be something important in there. If we're lucky he'll decide he should rush it down to the station."

"And if we're not lucky?"

They started up the wide stairs leading to the second floor. "Then, I'm going to have to get creative."

Agnes stopped at the top of the stairs, jerking to a halt. "Well, dangit!"

Flo's gaze followed Agnes' to the large form of Meanie Meldick hunkered down in a chair. His chin was on his well-padded chest, and Flo could hear his snores even from where they stood.

"It's okay, Agnes. He's asleep. We just need to be really quiet. We can get in and out before he wakes up."

Agnes frowned. "I don't know. What if he's a light sleeper?"

"If he wakes up, we'll just tell him we didn't want to bother him and that we put Mae's mail inside on her kitchen counter."

Agnes turned to Flo. "You think he's going to buy that?"

"Probably not, but the mail will be there and we're going to leave everything as it was when we went inside the apartment, so he's not going to be able to prove anything different.

Agnes sighed. "Okay. But if he wakes up, you do not have my permission to throw me at him as a distraction."

"Noted," Flo said, patting her friend on the back. "Let's go. Stay to the opposite side of the hallway, as far away from him as possible and *be quiet*."

Flo started down the hall, walking almost on her tippy-toes in an effort to escape the cranky officer's notice.

A particularly loud snore jolted them as they passed a small seating area. Agnes' arm jerked out, clipping the side of a table lamp and sending it toward the floor.

Flo dove toward the falling lamp, barely catching it before it landed. She glared at Agnes.

Agnes mouthed, "Sorry," and they moved on. They made it to the door without further mishap. Flo tried the door. Of course it was locked.

"Darn it!" Flo said in a frustrated whisper. "I don't suppose you have a lock pick set with you?"

Agnes snorted out a laugh. "Like either of us knows how to pick a lock, Flo. We could call TC or Celia?"

Flo lamented the fact that they hadn't brought the right members of their crew along on the job. She sighed. "I don't want to take the time. Meanie might wake up."

She looked around, seeing a small table beside the door with a pretty flowering plant in it. Flo lifted the pot, hoping Mae was careless enough with her key to have hidden it there.

No such luck.

Her gaze slid upward. She pointed to the doorframe. "Slide your fingers across the top of the frame and see if there's a key there."

Agnes did as requested, grimacing as her fingers dislodged an inch of dust and nothing else.

Flo was about to give up when she looked down and noticed the *Welcome* mat. Her gaze slid to Agnes'.

"It couldn't be that easy, could it?" Agnes asked.

"Only one way to find out," Flo said. She lifted the mat and saw nothing. "Well, it was worth a try..."

Agnes grabbed Flo's wrist, tugging upward. She grinned, pointing to the piece of brown shipping tape across the back of the mat. There was an unmistakable shape of a key beneath the tape.

"Eureka!" Flo whispered happily.

She quickly unlocked the door and let Agnes in first, then replaced the key and quietly closed the door. Flo leaned against the door for a moment, her heart pounding. Things were looking up.

She'd barely had the thought when a crash sounded from inside the apartment. Her eyes shot wide. *Agnes!* What had she been thinking letting the bull into the china shop without supervision?

She hurried down the hall, dodging the short wall where Roger had passed out, and bolting toward Agnes. "What happened?"

Agnes looked slowly up, her wide face dusted in white. She lifted her hands and they were coated in white powder too.

"What have you done?" Flo all but whined.

"It's not my fault, Flo. Somebody left the flour cannister at the edge of the counter. I bumped into it when I turned around."

Flo saw the telltale gray dust of a fingerprinting effort. "The police would have printed the whole kitchen. I' sure you're right and they didn't push it back into place." She shook her head. "But we can't leave this mess here. We need to clean it up."

Agnes nodded, running her hands down her jeans and leaving dual white tracks along her thighs. "I'll find a small vacuum. Can you pick up the big chunks of glass?"

Flo picked up a kitchen towel and used it to grab the bigger pieces of the clear glass cannister. "There's a lot of flour here, Agnes. You're going to need something bigger than a hand vac."

"Okay," Agnes called back from somewhere near the bathroom.

Silence suddenly filled the apartment. Flo got suspicious. "Agnes, what are you doing?"

Silence pulsed another minute. Finally, Agnes said, "I didn't touch it, Flo."

Flo straightened, dropping a large chunk of glass into the trash can. "Don't get distracted, Agnes." When her friend didn't respond, Flo sighed. She went to find out what kind of trouble Agnes was getting into.

She found her standing over the taped outline of Mae's body, staring at the large bloodstain. Agnes glanced up as Flo joined her. "That's a lot of blood."

Flo frowned. "Yes. Poor woman."

Agnes stood there without speaking for a long moment. Then she skimmed a narrowed glance toward Flo. "Roger couldn't have done this, right?"

Flo bit back the urge to yell at her friend. Agnes knew Roger almost as well as Flo did. She should know better. "Of course not! This is a brutal crime. Roger could never do this to anyone, let alone a defenseless woman."

"I don't know how defenseless she was, Flo. I mean, look at this place. She put up quite a fight."

Agnes was right. Flo had been too upset when she'd been there before to really notice much. But the apartment was a mess. Part of it likely had come from the police looking for evidence. But the furniture had been overturned when Flo and Roger had entered the apartment after Mae was already dead. "She did, didn't she?"

Agnes nodded, finally dragging herself from contemplation of the scene. "I'll go find the vacuum."

Flo nodded. As Agnes walked away, Flo realized she'd left flour tracks all around the scene. She closed her eyes and inhaled a deep, calming breath. It was her fault for bringing Agnes into the apartment with her. She'd been out of her mind. Agnes didn't mean any harm. But she was incapable of treading lightly through any space. And she had a particular skill for debauching crime scenes.

Flo knew this, and yet she'd brought her inside with her. It was a sure indication of how upset she was about Roger and how she wasn't thinking clearly.

The sound of wheels rolling across the carpet brought Flo's head up. Agnes rolled the vacuum past the bloodied couch and started toward the kitchen. "We'll need to vacuum in here too, Agnes. There's flour on the carpet."

"Oh. Okay." She changed direction, parking the vacuum in the middle of the living room and dragging the chord over to plug into the wall.

Flo stepped away. "You can handle this?"

"Of course, Flo," Agnes said with irritation in her tone. "I'm an adult woman. I think I know how to run a vacuum."

Flo bit back a snide response and nodded. "I'm going to look around. See if I can find anything mentioning Nicholai Pearce."

The vacuum started up behind Flo and she headed toward the bed and dressers, figuring it was the best place to start. It was doubtful Mae would have kept anything important in a kitchen drawer or cabinet. Unless she was paranoid, and the key taped to the Welcome mat said she wasn't.

Flo found nothing in the bedside table. Nothing under the mattress. And nothing in the larger dresser with the mirror. She'd even looked underneath all the drawers for something that might be taped there, given Mae's seeming love of taping stuff.

There was nothing.

Behind her, the vacuum stopped. She straightened, wiping her hands down her slacks, and looked at Agnes. "Done in there?"

Agnes nodded. "I think so. I need to pee."

"Look through the cabinets and inside the toilet tank while you're in there."

Agnes nodded, nearly dancing toward the apartment's only bathroom.

Flo went into the kitchen, taking care to step around the pile of flour. It was impossible to miss it all, though, the fine powder had blown around the room like an explosion when it hit the floor.

She found nothing in any of the cabinets and was looking inside the refrigerator when Agnes came back, dragging the vacuum into the kitchen behind her. "The bathroom was clean. Nothing with Pearce's name on it."

Flo was starting to lose hope they'd find anything. "I'm almost done here."

Agnes pulled the hose out of its slot in the vacuum and used it to suck up the worst of the flour. The machine made a terrible clanking sound as a large piece of glass was apparently sucked up with the flour.

Flo and Agnes shared a grimace.

It only took her a moment to search the nearly empty refrigerator. There was very little food in it. She tugged the freezer drawer open. Like the refrigerator, the freezer was mostly empty. She opened a couple of half gallons of ice cream and moved a few frozen pizzas aside to look underneath. She checked the drawers for taped additions and then straightened. Flo noticed a couple of receipts stuck to the side of the refrigerator with a heart-shaped magnet. They were for the new French café and another restaurant called *La Délicatesse*, which was in Indianapolis according to the address printed at the top of the receipt.

"Oops, I missed a spot," Agnes said.

Flo re-stuck the receipts to the side of the refrigerator as the vacuum started up again.

"Come on, Agnes. Let's get out of here..."

The vacuum screeched and made a loud clicking noise.

"Oh, oh," Agnes said.

Flo's stomach took a plunge. "Oh, no," she murmured, hurrying out of the kitchen,

Her lower half hidden by the short couch, Flo could see Agnes wrestling with the vacuum, her face a mask of horror.

"What's going on?" she asked as she hurried into the room. Her gaze was drawn downward, to the crime scene tape that was pulled taut, being steadily drawn into the sucking apparatus at the bottom of the vacuum. As Flo watched, the rest of the tape came free of the carpet and started to feed into the noisily gasping vacuum.

Agnes had her foot on the tape, attempting to keep it from entering the vacuum. She'd wrapped both hands around the handle, trying to yank the vacuum away from the tape.

With a yelp, Flo ran over and yanked the cord from the wall. She turned back. "Oh, Agnes. Look what you've done."

Agnes knelt down and started pulling on the tape. "It'll be all right. I'll just pull it out of here and reshape it. They'll never know."

Flo's knees went soft beneath her. There was no way Peters would miss the fact that his body outline had been uprooted and mangled into something unrecognizable.

She scrubbed a hand over her face. "Maybe we should just cut and run."

"No, Flo, I've got this. Here, just hold onto the tank like this..." Agnes fat-fingered the release button on top of the dust reservoir and it opened, spewing the contents of the reservoir all over the carpet.

Flo dropped her boohind into the nearest chair. "We're doomed."

CHAPTER EIGHT

Detective Brent Peters was too mad even to talk. He just stood there vibrating, his teeth grinding down to shiny white nubs. He lifted a hand and opened his mouth but seemed at a loss how to even begin.

For about the tenth time, he turned to Meanie Meldick and scoured him with an enraged glance.

Meanie shrank into himself, so compressed that he managed to look five hundred and fifty pounds rather than the usual six hundred.

Peters finally took a deep breath and looked at Flo, speaking to her as if she was dull. "Our. Agreement. Was. That. You." He paused to drag air into his lungs, presumably so he could continue on without drawing his weapon and shooting them. "Wouldn't. Interfere. With. My. Investigation."

She winced. "I know. I messed up. I'm really sorry. We just wanted to drop that mail off..." She pointed toward the pile of mail she'd left in plain view on the kitchen island.

Her apology seemed to throw him off for a beat. He was ready to do battle, his armor shined, his deadliest blade polished to a blinding sheen, and Flo was already waving the white flag.

She was trying to throw cool water on the conflagration that was his temper. And he didn't look happy about it. "I was trying to be understanding of your need to help Roger," he ground out past his newly nubbed teeth.

She nodded, crestfallen.

"I was trying to meet you halfway."

Flo sighed, staring at her hands.

"I didn't *think* I needed to tell you not to bring Wrecking Ball Willard to the crime scene."

"Hey!" Agnes objected.

Flo shook her head. "You're right. It was a huge mistake."

"Mistake!" Peters looked like he might spontaneously combust. "Mistake?" he repeated with heat. "Did you *look* at my crime scene?"

Flo lifted her head and winced as her gaze slid toward the mangled outline against her will. The body marker tape was twisted and blackened, popping up from the carpet in irregular bumps where the adhesive no longer held. Hair, dust, and flour stuck to the tacky side of the tape where it bulged upward, like giant tumors on the vaguely humanoid figure outlined on the rug. Agnes had managed to pull most of the tape out of the suction mechanism of the vacuum, but not all of it, so there were torn edges with gaps in the outline.

And the shape...all Flo could compare the bumpy, misshapen mess to was a turtle climbing a tree...with balloons in one paw.

"I agree the shape is wrong. But the basic location is still right," she tried.

"The basic location!" he roared, seemingly before he could stop himself. Barely reining himself in, Peters lifted a hand, continuing in a too-soft voice that somehow managed to be worse than the shouting. "The blood spatter is four feet away." His lips drew back from his teeth. "Under that pile of dust and flour."

Flo finally realized she wasn't going to fix anything by speaking. Trying would be as futile as attempting to convince the people in a town that was near a volcano, whose buildings were totally flattened by lava, that the bubbling inferno covering their homes represented a great opportunity to redecorate. She pressed her lips together and just let the verbal beating pound into her. Flo listened as Agnes accepted her own verbal assault, fortunately without much comment. And she squirmed in her chair as poor Meanie took his vocal scalding.

Twenty minutes later, Flo and Agnes scuttled out of the apartment with their tails between their legs and hit the hallway at a near run.

"Well, that wasn't so bad," Agnes said, grinning.

Flo looked at her in amazement, mouth hanging open.

"What's next?" Agnes asked.

"What's next?" Flo repeated in a soft shriek.

Agnes' eyes went wide. "Is there an echo in here?"

Flo shook her head. "What's next is that I'm going to take Rodney for a walk, and then I'm going to go see Roger." She frowned. "Don't you have an engagement dinner or something tonight with Hertz?"

Agnes nodded, not looking very happy about it. "At least I have a cool dress to wear."

Flo couldn't argue with that. They parted ways at the elevators. Flo headed toward her apartment as Agnes climbed one more floor to hers.

Before she got to her door, Flo remembered what Elisa Kemp had told her about Cook. She changed direction and headed downstairs. If she was lucky, she'd find Cook in the dining room, planning the meals for the following day.

COOK WAS STANDING AT the short railing dividing the bar from the dining room. She was chatting it up with Dutch, Silver Hills' bartender.

The big man was telling her a story that had her chuckling, the deep sound pleasantly familiar.

Flo waved at Dutch and climbed up onto a tall stool near the dividing wall. "Join me for a minute?" she asked Cook.

The plus-sized Cajun nodded. "Be happy to, *cher*."

"What can I get ya, Mrs. Bee?" Dutch asked in his gruff voice.

"I'll take a hot tea, please. With lemon."

Cook settled herself onto the stool opposite Flo with a groan. "Busy morning, *cher*. Busy morning."

"I'll bet. The residence is full up. There isn't even a studio apartment available right now." As soon as she said the words, Flo regretted them. Actually, there was one studio available. Thanks to a brutal killer.

"You've been lookin' inta Mae Caldone's death?" Cook asked, sipping her glass of what looked like sparkling water.

Flo nodded, thanking Dutch for the tea he placed in front of her. "Elisa told me you spoke to her."

Cook's big head bobbed up and down. She scribbled on her meal-planning pad with her pencil, her expression thoughtful.

"I been tryin' ta remember who dat woman was who was fightin' wid Pearce. I tink I finally placed her." She looked up into Flo's gaze. "I seen her at dat new restaurant downtown. She was talking to da guy in charge dere."

"Which restaurant," Flo asked, sipping her tea.

"Dat new one. Da Bistro?"

"Le Petite Bistro," Flo nodded. "We ate there yesterday. It was good." Flo couldn't believe it had only been a day. So much had happened in less than twenty-four hours.

"I been meanin' ta get dere. I plan ta try it out on my day off."

"So, you think you saw this woman with the owner? What do you mean *saw* her? As in talking to him?"

"Dey was talkin' yeah, *cher*. But dey was makin' eyes too. You know what I mean?"

"Like they were in a relationship?" Flo asked

Cook shrugged. "Mebbe. Or wanted ta be."

Ah! Things were getting more interesting by the minute. Had Pearce put the moves on François' wife? That would certainly be motive for François to kill Pearce. But why kill poor Mae? Still, it was an interesting development in the investigation.

"What did she look like?" Flo asked.

"Tiny ting. Hair so blonde it was white. Pretty like a fashion doll." Cook grimaced slightly as if that wasn't a compliment.

"You think she looked plastic?" Flo asked, curious.

"Yeah. Dat girl wore too much makeup and not enough clothes."

Flo nodded. "Thanks, Cook. That might be helpful information. If you see her again, will you let me know?"

The big woman nodded. "How's poor Roger?"

Guilt swam through her. She'd forgotten her intention to go see him. "I haven't been over there yet. I'm going to go in a few minutes, after I walk Rodney."

TC found her as she took Rodney out to the yard to do his business. "I was hoping I'd see you out here. I'm going to see Roger. Do you want to come along?"

Flo nodded. "I'd love to. I was planning on going after Rodney finished his business."

TC eyed her carefully. "Rough day?"

"You have no idea." She sighed. "Your boyfriend's going to give you an earful about it, but the short story is that Agnes debauched another of his crime scenes."

To Flo's shock, humor sparkled in TC's green gaze. "What did she do this time?"

"She vacuumed up the body marker."

TC burst into laughter, shaking her head. "Agnes is a force of nature. I keep telling Brent you can't control forces of nature."

"That's one way to look at it," Flo groused. "He yelled at all of us for twenty minutes. Poor Meanie Meldick will probably never speak to us again."

Her eyes went wide. "Meanie let you into the apartment?"

"Not on purpose. He fell asleep and we tiptoed past him."

TC's grin widened. "I'm trying to imagine Agnes tiptoeing past anything."

Flo couldn't suppress a grin of her own. "Meanie's a very heavy sleeper."

"Well," TC glanced at her watch. "How soon will you be ready to go? I promised mom I'd be over to watch old movies with her."

TC's mom had Alzheimer's and, like other victims of the disease, she had good days and bad. TC was continuing a tradition in their family of watching movies from the past as her mother had watched classic movies with her mother. She said the movies calmed her mother and made her happy.

"I'm ready now. If you don't mind taking Rodney along."

"No, that's fine. He can terrorize everybody who walks past the car in the parking lot."

Flo chuckled. "You sure know how to make a Dachshund's day, hun."

THEY STOPPED AT THE nurse's station on Roger's floor and got directions to his room.

The woman was busy but seemed friendly. "He's a popular guy today."

"What do you mean?" TC asked.

"He's got company in there right now."

"It's probably Richard," Flo told her friend.

TC nodded and they headed toward Roger's room.

Flo would have never in a million years expected the man who exited Roger's room as they approached.

Nicholai Pearce's attractive face was dark, the heavy slash of eyebrows lowered over eyes that were filled with rage. His steps were quick, his gait stiff, and he skimmed to a stop when he saw them as if they'd pulled a weapon on him.

Pearce lifted a hand, jabbing the air in front of Flo with a finger. "You tell him I'm not done with him. I know what he did. He's not going to get away with it."

Flo was speechless. She and TC watched the man stalk toward the elevator and disappear inside, his angry scowl the last thing they saw of him before the doors slid closed.

Flo looked at TC. "What in the world just happened?"

TC shook her head. "I have no idea. But we'd better check on Roger."

They found him sitting up in bed, twisting his long fingers together as he stared out the window on the other side of the room.

His head whipped around as they entered the room, his gaze filled with surprise when he saw them.

"Roger, what in the world...?"

He held up a hand as if to stop her. "Don't ask me. I have no idea. The man marched in here and started screaming. If that little nurse hadn't come in and told him to leave, I think he might have started pounding on me. Nicholai Pearce has a terrible temper."

"Nurse?" Flo asked, looking around.

Roger frowned toward the door. "She shooed him out and left. But he turned around and came back for one, last shot."

"What did he say to you?" TC asked, dropping into one of the chairs beside Roger's bed.

"Crazy stuff." Roger shook his head. "First he accused me of sending the police after him. I told him the police were more interested in looking at me for that young woman's death than him."

"How'd he react to that?"

"He said, 'Good!'" Roger let his confusion show as he looked at Flo. "The man actually believes I killed Mae Caldone." Roger's voice was filled with such disbelief, if Flo'd had any concerns that he was guilty, his confusion would have gone a long way toward convincing her otherwise. "Why would I kill her?"

TC reached out and took his hand, stilling the twisting fingers. "You wouldn't. And we're going to prove you didn't."

Flo nodded. "We're already investigating." Flo had a thought. "Roger, you've spent some time with Pearce lately, haven't you?"

Roger nodded. "A bit. We played poker. I took him around the place, introducing him and showing him the ropes." He shrugged. "Same as I do with any new person who seems to want the tour."

"Did you ever see him with a petite woman with white-blonde hair. She might have been wearing too much makeup and too little clothing." Flo flushed when she offered the final bit of detail, knowing Roger would be reluctant to speak ill of some woman he didn't know and also knowing she wouldn't be happy to know he'd noticed.

He shook his head. "Pearce never talked about women. He noticed them just fine. But he didn't share his thoughts on the subject."

"Given what we've heard about him, that seems out of character," Flo said.

"What have you heard?" Roger asked.

"That he's a womanizer. And, before her death, Mae admitted to me he'd been too possessive and kind of forceful with her."

Roger frowned. "Why does that lead you to believe he'd talk to me about women?"

"I don't know. I thought men talked about those things to each other." Flo couldn't very well tell Roger she thought of Pearce's behavior as being very Alpha male, and she thought that type of man bragged about his conquests. She was aware her perceptions could be seen as old-fashioned and out of touch. But she was more worried Roger would see them as a conviction that she saw him as being weaker somehow because of his gentle kindness.

Nothing could be further from the truth.

"We talked about poker at the card game and Silver Hills during the tour. Other than that, we haven't really spoken."

They wouldn't have had much time. Mae was murdered mere days after Pearce arrived.

"How's your head?" Flo asked.

"It's killing me," Roger grumped. "I'd try to sleep it off, but the dang nurses keep waking me up to check this and test that." He shook his head. "Whoever thought hospitals were a good place for people to get better was seriously confused about the whole healing process."

Flo and TC shared a look. It was unlike Roger to be so crabby, but Flo knew from personal experience how much a concussion headache hurt. Even a minor one.

She noticed Roger rubbing a couple of bloody tracks on the inside of one arm. "What happened to your arm?"

He glanced at it, lifting his fingers away. "I don't know. I must have scratched it on the corner of the table when I fell."

"Table?" Flo's eyes went wide. "You remember falling on a table?"

He turned to her, surprise filling his blue gaze. "I do. Well, isn't that something? I guess my memory's coming back." He didn't necessarily look happy about it.

For the first time, Flo wondered if Roger was afraid to remember what had happened in Mae Caldone's apartment.

She shoved that thought aside. It was a ridiculous notion. "Do you remember how or why you fell?"

Roger seemed to consider it for a moment and then shook his head. "No. I've got nothing."

A knocking sound had them all turning toward the man standing just outside the door. Detective Brent Peters smiled at TC, but his smile fell away when he spotted Flo. "Ladies, could I have a moment, please?"

"Of course." Thinking he wanted to speak to Roger, Flo was surprised when he followed them a distance down the hall.

"What's up?" TC asked.

"I heard you asking Roger about those scratches," Peters said, his expression unreadable. Something in the way he held himself had Flo's warning bells clanging.

"He thinks he scratched his arm falling on a table," Flo told the cop. "Was there any evidence of that at the scene?"

Peters gave her a look. "If there had been, I'm sure your buddy would have vacuumed it. Or thrown-up on it. Or dropped an entire bag of flour on top of it."

Flo winced. She'd deserved that. "I *said* I was sorry about that whole thing," she tried again.

Peters shook his head. "It's done. We'll just have to work around it. What I wanted to tell you was that the Medical Examiner found DNA under Mae Caldone's fingernails." He held Flo's gaze and her pulse spiked.

Flo wasn't the only one who saw trouble coming. TC reached over and clasped Flo's hand, her nails digging into the skin of her palm.

Clang! Warning bells were banging around in Flo's head loud enough for everyone near her to hear them. "Okay..."

Flo was aware she should ask where Peters was going with that little nugget of info.

She should.

But she wasn't sure she could bring herself to do it.

"We also got a DNA sample from Roger Attles after he was admitted here."

Clang, clang, clang, clang...

TC broke first. "What are you trying to tell us, Brent? Spit it out."

"Roger's DNA was a match for the genetic material under Mae Caldone's nails," he said, watching for Flo's reaction. "Those scratches on his arm were from the victim."

CHAPTER NINE

"It's not possible," Flo told her friends at the breakfast table the next morning. She'd lain awake most of the night, worrying about what Detective Peters had told them. "Roger couldn't have hurt that young woman."

Agnes swallowed a bit of French toast and nodded. "I agree. There's got to be some other explanation."

Flo tried not to think about her friend's destruction of the crime scene. If Agnes' stomping all over the scene had managed to smudge vital evidence that would clear Roger... She sighed. Agnes hadn't meant to do it, and she wasn't about to make her feel guilty about it. "Of course there is and we're going to find it," she said.

"How are we going to do that?" TC asked. "There's no way Brent's going to let us back inside that apartment."

"We're going to find the real killer," Flo replied.

"Do you have any ideas about that?" Ce asked, settling her teacup into its saucer.

"A couple. Cook told me she saw Pearce fighting with a young woman at the market. She said the woman looked familiar."

"She knew her?" Agnes asked.

"No. But she'd apparently seen her with François Liberte before."

Celia's eyes went wide. "François as in Le Petite Bistro François?"

"The same one," Flo agreed, nodding. "She also said Mae was overheard in the gym here at Silver Hills arguing with some guy about pestering her. If we can get a description of that guy, we might have another suspect to give the police."

"Who overheard her?" TC asked.

"Renee Woldigger."

TC frowned. "I think Renee's in my Zumba class this afternoon. You should come to the class and talk to her."

Flo grimaced. "I'm not good at Zumba. My brain can't figure out the steps that fast."

"I have some moves," Ce told her friends, looking a tiny bit smug.

"I'm great at it," Agnes said, grinning. "It's a good workout."

"Good, I'll see you all there at two o'clock then," TC said, nodding.

"Elisa's checking into the museum date alibi Pearce gave us," Flo told her friends. "Hopefully, the woman he was supposed to have been with is fictitious, and we can blow that out of the water."

"How are we going to find the woman Cook described," Agnes asked.

"I guess it could be François' wife," Celia said. "Sophia's hair is blonde, I wouldn't call it white though. Her makeup can be dramatic at times." Ce frowned. "The Libertes have two kids. I really hope we're not going to find out he's been sleeping around."

"Hopefully not," Flo agreed. "But we need to rule that out. If we find out Pearce has been sleeping with the same woman, we have a whole new set of possibilities for Mae's murder."

"Like what?" Agnes asked, frowning. "What would any of that have to do with Mae?"

"I don't know yet," Flo admitted. "Jealousy maybe? Or blackmail? We need to paint the whole picture surrounding her death before we can see the brush strokes of Mae's murder."

"Very poetic, Flo," TC said, giving Flo's arm a gentle nudge. "I might steal it for one of my books."

"Thanks," Flo said, grinning. "I try. And steal away. As long as you don't create a character with my name and kill her off, I'm happy to be an inspiration."

They parted ways, with TC promising to get Renee Woldigger's room number just in case she didn't show up for Zumba, and Celia offering to ask Mass about François Liberte's character and associations.

Flo glanced at her watch. It was ten o'clock in the morning. They had hours to kill before Zumba. She decided to head to the office and see if she could get Renee's room number from Richard. Then she remembered that Richard was probably still at the hospital. Which meant she'd probably have to deal with the night manager. Otherwise known as the resident bloodsucker.

She sighed.

"HOW'D YOUR DINNER GO last night?" Flo asked Agnes as they headed across the lobby. She glanced toward her friend in time to see Agnes wince. "What's wrong?"

Agnes never got a chance to respond.

The office door opened and something cold and oily oozed out. High overhead, the lobby lights flickered. The music being piped through the common area speakers stuttered as if touched by a fault in the electrical system.

Flo and Agnes skidded to a stop a few feet away from the bloodsucker who'd stopped just outside the door to lock his black gaze on them. The look was filled with accusation.

Flo had no idea what Vladwicke Newsome, a.k.a. Vlad, would accuse them of. It could be anything from clogging the building's ancient plumbing with tissues, to disturbing the peace with their respective pets.

Whatever it was, Flo would take it with a drop of...erm...blood. The night manager at Silver Hills held no fondness for Flo or Agnes.

The feeling was definitely mutual.

"Vlad," Flo said, putting an extra sliver of wood into her voice in the hopes it would turn him to ash.

His response was to curl one thin lip. He turned his gaze to Agnes. "I understand there was a mix-up in the kitchen over the weekend."

The tone of his statement made it very clear that, in his opinion, Agnes was to be blamed for the problem. Technically, if there was a problem to be handled on the weekends, as Weekend Manager, Agnes was the person responsible. But Vlad was fully capable of making her the villain in any situation.

Agnes shrugged. "We ran out of potatoes. It was no big deal. Natashia made rice and almost everybody was happy."

Almost, because cranky Old Mrs. Peoples was loud and energetic with her complaints. But since the surly nonagenarian also complained about everything else having to do with the meal, Flo thought her opinions could be safely discounted.

"The rice was delicious," Flo told Vlad. "I didn't hear anybody complaining."

Vlad's lip curled higher, showing a hint of fang. "I don't believe I asked for your opinion, Mrs. Bee."

"No, I don't believe you did," Flo told him. "Aren't you lucky I gave it anyway?"

Much gnashing of fangs followed her statement. Flo fought to restrain a smug grin.

"I'm assuming you spoke to young Natasha about planning better in the future?"

Flo happened to know Agnes had done no such thing. She'd offered to run to the store to get more potatoes instead. A much more productive response in Flo's opinion. But if she told Vlad she hadn't, he'd take it upon himself to drain the sweet young woman of any happiness he could suction away. So, Agnes did the smart thing.

She lied.

"Of course. Natasha understands her mistake and won't make it again. But in her defense, we had a much larger crowd than usual. Word is getting out in Silver City about the quality of our restaurant. People who don't live here are coming to eat now. Unless you want to cut that source of revenue, I don't see a way around occasionally running out of food. The key is in how we handle it when that happens," Agnes told him, sounding like a CEO running a board meeting.

Flo covered a grin with her hand, not wanting to antagonize the blood-sucker for fear he'd take it out on Agnes.

Vlad narrowed his mean gaze on Agnes, clearly at a loss for a response, and then lifted onto his toes as if he was considering turning into a bat and flying away. He crossed his hands behind his back and leaned forward as if his narrow black shoes were nailed to the ground. "See that it doesn't happen again. Your little weekend gig is not guaranteed."

They watched him float away, their moods soured by the encounter.

If a woman could produce actual steam, Flo was pretty sure Agnes would have some of the stuff streaming from her ears. "He's such a jerk."

And Flo had been so distracted by Vlad's full-frontal assault she'd forgotten to ask him about Renee's address.

Not that he would have given it to her anyway.

Flo patted her friend's arm. "Never mind him. You really got him with that revenue source comment." Flo chuckled. "He didn't know what to do with it."

Agnes smiled. "It's true. Our weekend restaurant business has quadrupled since Cook decided to take a couple of days off and gave Natasha a shot at being chef. People really seem to like her Eastern European take on things."

"Morning, ladies!" A familiar voice called out.

They turned to find Hertz Thompson heading their way. His round cheeks were flushed and he was walking briskly, coming from the direction of the front door. He reached them and bent to peck Agnes on the cheek.

Agnes flushed with embarrassment.

"You've been out and about already?" Flo asked with a smile.

"I have. I'm walking two miles a day now." He wrapped an arm around Agnes' waist. "I'm trying to get my best girl to join me, but mostly she's been resisting." He gave Agnes a look that seemed to hold some secret meaning, making Agnes squirm.

Flo blew a raspberry. "Don't hold your breath on that, Hertz. Not unless you have extremely good lungs. Agnes has been resisting that type of exercise as long as I've known her."

He chuckled. "I'm a patient man. And a stubborn one." Again, his comment seemed be saying something beyond what it seemed to say.

Flo couldn't help noticing how uncomfortable Hertz's conversation was making Agnes. To change the subject, she nodded to the paper sack in his hand. "I see you stopped at the farmer's market."

Nodding, he indicated the bag with a jerk of his chin. "Not much there this time of year. I got some apples, kale and wild mushrooms. It's the last week and I wanted to make sure I had one last hurrah."

Agnes grimaced when he mentioned the kale. "Ugh! I hope you're using my recipe for that stuff."

Hertz gave her a crooked smile. "I can't wait to hear this. What is your recipe for kale, Aggie?"

Agnes flushed a deep red at the nickname. "You take a frying pan, put some oil in the bottom, add the kale and swish it around a bit. Then walk over to the trash and dump it in. The kale slides right out of the pan into the trash. Close lid. Serves zero people, and that's as it should be."

Flo and Hertz laughed.

"Maybe I should walk down to the market myself," Flo said. "Rodney needs a walk anyway, and I wouldn't mind getting some apples and greens."

"There was a vendor selling pumpkin and cinnamon scented homemade soaps too," Hertz said, smiling. "I love homemade soap."

Flo decided a walk was just the ticket and excused herself. Rodney would be in heaven. And it would give her time to consider her next move in the investigation.

TEN MINUTES LATER, Flo was striding down the sidewalk, inhaling the crisp, clean smell of an early winter day and enjoying the warm sun on her face. As predicted, Rodney was beside himself with joy. He bounced along on his stubby legs, tail whipping happily behind him as he forged a path down the sidewalk. No blowing scrap of paper or waving blade of grass was safe from the little dog's excited attentions as they covered the quarter mile distance to the Non-denominational church parking lot where the weekly farmer's market was held.

Rodney snagged a random receipt that tried to blow past and carried it along with him, head held high with pride as if the thin scrap covered in smeared ink was the greatest treasure.

Flo shook her head at her little man, grinning as she felt some of the tension of the last twenty-four hours draining away.

"Mrs. Bee?"

She turned to find Reverend Huckleberry standing on the sidewalk leading from the front doors of Emmanuel Lutheran Church. He was wearing jeans and a yellow button-up shirt underneath a Notre Dame jacket. His thick mop of iron-gray hair curled around the edges of a baseball cap bearing the Indianapolis Colts' logo.

She stopped and gave him a smile. "Hello, Reverend. How are you?"

He descended two concrete steps and took her hand, giving it a squeeze. "I'm just fine, young lady. I won't ask how you are. I see the bounce in your step and the roses in your cheeks."

Flo laughed. "The cool air and sunshine are doing wonders for my disposition."

Rodney barked enthusiastically as if in agreement. He waddled over and sniffed the Reverend's white sneakers, eyes bright and tail wagging.

"Well, hello there, young man. You're looking bright-eyed today too."

Flo and the Reverend had bonded over their love of dachshunds. Reverend Huckleberry had two of the little dogs. A dapple long-haired female named Sissy and a short-haired black and tan male named George. The Reverend had lost his wife from cancer the year previous and had told Flo his little dogs had helped him keep his sanity when missing her had almost done him in.

"How are your little guys?"

"Ornery as always," he said, grinning. "They're so much company. I don't know what I'd do without them."

"I couldn't agree more."

"Are you heading to the Farmer's Market?" the reverend asked.

"I am."

"I was heading there myself. Do you mind if I walk with you?"

"I'd love the company."

They walked in companionable silence for a moment, the reverend greeting people they passed on the street. About a block from the market, he turned to her with a frown. "I understand you're looking into Mae Caldone's death."

Flo bit back the urge to clarify it as a murder. Some people took comfort in vague language where things like murder were involved.

"Yes. You knew Mae?"

"She came to services at Emmanuel Lutheran. Nearly every Sunday."

Flo was surprised by that. Mae Caldone hadn't seemed like a spiritual person. Though Flo hadn't really known her well enough to judge for sure. "I didn't know."

He inclined his head, thoughtful. "She actually came to me a few days ago looking for guidance on a personal matter."

Flo turned to him, catching his eye. "And you think whatever the personal matter was, it might help me find her killer?"

He compressed his lips at the word "killer" but nodded. "Of course, you know I wouldn't share her private business if she were still alive. But given the situation, I believe Mae would want me to tell you what she told me."

Flo nodded toward a bench a distance from the bustling market. "Shall we sit for a minute?"

They settled onto the bench together. Reverend Huckleberry leaned his head back with a sigh, closing his eyes. "I wish it could stay like this all winter."

"That would be wonderful." She didn't push. She let him come to his intended point in his own time. Watching Rodney chase a leaf blowing across the sidewalk, Flo tried to guess what Mae had told the pastor.

Nothing she guessed was even close.

Reverend Huckleberry opened his eyes and fixed an intense gaze on Flo. "Miss Caldone said she was afraid because she'd seen something. Something she shouldn't have. And she felt as if someone was watching her."

Flo turned a surprised glance on him. "Did she say what she'd seen?"

"No. I wish now that she had. I'd love to be able to point a finger at the person who killed her."

"What else did she say?"

"Only that she'd had a disagreement with a man recently who had power and standing in the community. Someone knowledgeable about the law. And she thought maybe he was going to hurt her."

Flo's stomach twisted with alarm. "Like a police officer?"

"No. I didn't get the impression we were talking about the police. More like a lawyer, maybe?"

Her world swayed. Flo fought sudden vertigo, clamping a hand on the armrest of the wooden bench.

Reverend Huckleberry noticed. "Mrs. Bee? Are you okay?"

She shook her head. "No. I'm not. You knew Roger Attles had been hurt when Mae was killed?"

"I'd heard that, yes." His expression cleared as he seemed to realize the connection. "You and Mr. Attles are good friends."

"Yes. And the police are looking at him as a suspect." She held his gaze, willing him to make the connection.

His eyes went wide. "He's a lawyer."

Flo nodded, her eyes filling with tears. "Roger wouldn't kill anyone. Let alone a woman."

"I'm inclined to agree with you. From everything I know about him, Mr. Attles is a gentleman."

Flo heard the "but" in his words. She knew what he was thinking. People were always fooled by what their loved ones and acquaintances were capable of. How many times had she heard a relative or neighbor of a killer proclaim on the news how kind and wonderful the person was?

"He couldn't have done it," she said again, in answer to the accusation the Reverend wouldn't voice.

His gaze softened as he patted her arm. "I'm sure you're right. And he's lucky to have you in his corner, Mrs. Bee."

She sniffed, scrubbing a hand over her cheeks. "I'd best be going now." She stood, forcing a smile. "It was nice visiting with you."

The reverend looked as though he wanted to say something else, but didn't, finally nodding. "I'll see you soon."

CHAPTER TEN

Flo walked briskly toward the market. Her mind raced with questions and worry. What if the killer turned out to be a lawyer like Roger? The coincidence was just too big for the police to overlook.

Despite her original plan to get some fresh produce, Flo realized her conversation with the reverend had killed her interest in shopping. She wandered aimlessly past the booths for a while, noting that some of them were already shutting down for the day. And, probably the season.

A shrill laugh drew her attention to a young woman standing behind a table covered in a pretty array of soaps.

The woman was bent double, eyeing Rodney from underneath the table.

To Flo's unending horror, her little dog was peeing on one of the woman's table legs. "Oh, my goodness! I'm so sorry." She hurried over to grab Rodney. "I'll go get something to clean that up."

The woman straightened to her full height, which wasn't much. She looked to be even shorter than Flo, and that was saying something. She was smiling, her brown eyes crinkling at the corners as if she smiled often. "Don't be silly. Puppies do what puppies do." She reached behind her and grabbed a spray bottle. "I bring this for emergencies. You'd be surprised how often this happens." The woman walked around front and spritzed the table leg Rodney had anointed. "There. Good as new." She shoved a glossy strand of silvery blonde hair behind one ear, grinning down at the happy-go-lucky dachshund. "All better, handsome."

Rodney barked, his tail whipping the air. He ran over and sniffed her shoes and then bounced around and barked again.

"He likes you," Flo said. "He doesn't generally like strangers." The woman reminded her of someone, but she couldn't recall who. She thought the vendor was probably in her late thirties. She was pretty but would be prettier with less makeup.

"Stranger danger," the woman said in a baby voice to Rodney. "Good boy! Stay away from strangers." Her smile slipped slightly. She looked at Flo with some embarrassment, her pale cheeks flushing. "I'm sorry. I miss my little Yorkie. She's staying with my parents until I can find a place that will let me keep a dog."

"Oh, hun. That must be awful. If I didn't have this little man, I don't know what I'd do."

The woman nodded, her expression sad. But she didn't seem to be the type of person to wallow. She forced a bright smile a moment later. "Can I interest you in some homemade soap?"

Flo was on the verge of saying no, but then it fell into place why the other woman seemed familiar. "Show me what you have. I actually love homemade soap."

The vendor clapped her hands. "Me too! I'll tell you a little secret. I used to work as an exotic dancer in Indianapolis." She made a face. "Still do part-time. But I'm trying to open a shop here in Silver City to sell my soaps and homemade cosmetics."

"I love that idea. I'll definitely come to your shop. We don't have anything like that in Silver City. If I like your soaps, I'll talk you up to the other residents at Silver Hills."

Her gaze widened. "You live there? Such a pretty building. I drive by there all the time and wish I could live in a place like that."

"You could, hun," Flo said. "Why not?"

She shrugged. "I actually think I'm going to look for an old storefront with an apartment above it. That way I'll only have one rent payment every month."

"That makes perfect sense." Flo thought about the storefront where Mayor Potts had run his campaign. "I think I know just the place. I don't know if it's available, but the last time I drove past the *For-Rent* sign was still up."

"Where is it?" the young woman asked.

Flo gave her the street and the building description. She wrote it on the back of a receipt. "Mayor Potts ran his campaign from there. There's a really nice enclosed room upstairs, with a bathroom and a small kitchenette. It might be perfect if you're not looking for something fancy."

"It sounds wonderful! Thanks for this." She held the receipt in the air and offered Flo her hand. "I'm Bonnie Feckle."

"Florence Bee. My friends call me Flo."

"Flo it is then." Bonnie turned to her table, perusing the variety of colors, shapes, and sizes of chunky soaps. "What scent do you like?"

"I'm partial to lavender," Flo told her, walking over to look at the selection.

Bonnie plucked a lavender-colored block from the selection, wrapped it in pretty tissue paper, and handed it to Flo. "It's on the house. As a thank you for helping me find a place."

"Oh, hun. You don't need to do that."

"I want to."

"Okay, but I'd like to look at the rest. I'm thinking these would make great Christmas gifts."

Fifteen minutes later, Bonnie handed Flo a bag bulging with soaps, lotions, and a couple of woven soap cozies that Flo couldn't wait to try. She was trying to think how to broach the subject of Nicholai Pearce when Bonnie gave her the opening she needed.

"There was a murder at Silver Hills recently, wasn't there?" Something skimmed through the other woman's gaze that made Flo wonder at the reason for her question. It could be morbid curiosity, but Bonnie hadn't seemed the type to indulge in that.

"There was. A woman named Mae Caldone. Did you know her?"

The brown gaze widened slightly before Bonnie glanced away, shaking her head. "Do the police have a suspect yet?"

Watching her carefully, Flo nodded. "They're taking a good look at a man named Nicholai Pearce. He was apparently dating Mae and had been...aggressive is probably the right word. I saw them fighting on the sidewalk in front of Le Petite Bistro myself."

"Fighting? Really? What about?"

"I have no idea. I was across the street. I only noticed because I recognized Mr. Pearce from Silver Hills."

Her gaze went wide again. Bonnie Feckle was certainly no poker face. "Oh my! I didn't realize he'd moved in there."

Flo stared at the woman, waiting for her to realize her mistake. A beat later, she closed her eyes, expelling a sigh. Flo decided to help her along. "You know Nicholai Pearce, don't you?"

The young woman chewed her bottom lip. "We've met."

When Bonnie didn't elaborate, Flo gave her another verbal nudge. "You knew him well enough to argue with him right here at this market, didn't you?"

Bonnie's gaze narrowed with suspicion. "Who told you that?"

Flo dug out one of her business cards and handed it to the other woman. "I'm investigating Mae's death."

Bonnie expelled a frustrated stream of air. "I'm such a putz. You didn't just happen to stop by today, did you?"

"I actually did. I was just wandering around, intending to do a little shopping. But when I saw you, I realized you fit the description of someone who was seen arguing with Pearce here at the market."

Bonnie shook her head, staring at Flo's card.

"I'm not trying to point the finger at you for murder, Bonnie. I'm just looking for the truth. I need to find out what really happened."

Bonnie's head lifted. She fixed Flo with an assessing look. "Why are you involved, Mrs. Bee?"

"Flo, please."

Bonnie shook her head, frowning slightly. It was clear she believed Flo had ambushed her.

"To be honest, Bonnie," Flo said in a gentle tone. "I'm worried about a friend. Someone who I believe was just in the wrong place at the wrong time and who's now under suspicion for Mae's murder."

Bonnie's mulish expression softened. "I'm sorry to hear that."

Flo nodded. "I'm not lying to you, Bonnie. I'm just trying to get to the truth."

The other woman sighed. "I do know Nic. He and I have dated a few times. And, yes, I've been talking to him about doing business together."

Flo's brows lifted. "Business?"

"He's interested in being an *investor*."

The way she said the word gave Flo a clue that Bonnie wasn't in the least interested. "Is he..." Flo struggled to find a non-inflammatory word for what she wanted to ask and failed. "Is he being difficult about your obvious lack of interest in partnering?"

Bonnie laughed harshly. "You could say that, yes. Nic isn't a big fan of hard work and building from the ground up. He's all about making the fast buck, finding shortcuts to success. We wouldn't be compatible business partners."

"Shortcuts to success? Like what, specifically?"

Bonnie fixed her with an angry look. "Like running over anybody who gets in your way. Like mowing them down if necessary. And forcing them to comply when nothing else works."

"Do you believe Pearce is capable of hurting someone?" Flo asked just to clarify.

"Absolutely."

"Do you believe he might have killed Mae Caldone?"

She shrugged. "I didn't know Mae. I have no idea what their relationship was like. But if it's as you've said...that he was being aggressive with her in a romantic capacity...then, yes. Pearce's first, last and driving goal is always to get what he wants. If Mae stood in the way of that, I have no doubt he'd do whatever he needed to do to remove her as an obstacle."

"MRS. BEE, CAN I HAVE a word, please?"

Flo turned to the person hailing her from behind. She'd left Bonnie's booth and headed straight out of the market, her mind spinning with questions. As she turned to see who was calling her, she had the sense that the woman hurrying up to her had called out several times before Flo had heard.

She got that impression mostly from the fact that Nanna Potts looked decidedly irritated.

"Hey, Nanna. How are you?"

Flo almost didn't recognize the woman hurrying toward her She looked like she'd lost some weight, and she wore a crisp business suit as befitted the right-hand lady of the city's mayor.

Mayor Potts' mother and campaign manager slash adviser forced a smile that she clearly didn't feel. "I've been better. Can we walk and talk?" She skimmed a glance around the area as if making sure she couldn't be overheard.

"Of course." They fell into step on the sidewalk. Flo was forced to walk more quickly than usual to keep up with the energetic Nanna.

Down by her feet, Rodney gave a little growl, no doubt affected by the negative vibes coming off Nanna. Or just irritated that his leisurely exploration of the world around him was being rushed.

"How are the boys?" Flo asked after a moment. Nanna's two sons, David Junior and Peter, affectionately known as Pet, were both smart, accomplished young men whom Flo had taught during her years as a substitute teacher.

Nanna nodded almost absent-mindedly. "They're good. They're fine."

"Young Peter should be graduating in the spring, right?"

"Yes," she frowned. "Pet's doing well." She turned to Flo. "Look, I need to get something straight with you." Shoving a hand into her shiny cap of hair, Nanna stopped walking and turned to fix a slightly hostile gaze on Flo. "My personal life is my business. I don't like people digging around in it."

Flo was at a loss. "I don't understand..."

Nanna huffed out a sigh. "I went to Indianapolis with Nicholai Pearce. I was his date for the evening. I know you've had your gossip hound looking into it, and I want it to stop."

Flo felt her eyes go wide. "*You're* his alibi?"

Nanna's light hazel gaze swung away. "Apparently, yes."

Flo thought about that for a moment. She'd known Nanna Potts for a long time. Not as a friend, but as someone who'd taught Nanna's kids and occasionally spent time with her at school functions. She would have never thought the other woman was Nicholai Pearce's type. Though Nanna hadn't really shown great taste in men in the past. Her deceased husband, David Potts, had been a hard man to like.

But dating a player... That didn't seem smart on so many levels.

Then Flo thought about the meeting at Le Petite Bistro. "That's why Pearce met with David."

Nanna's face flushed with anger or embarrassment. Flo wasn't sure which.

"It seems my son thinks my personal life is his business too."

Flo suddenly understood Nanna's anger. Her relationships, however ill-advised, *were* her own business. Unless she was shielding a killer. "I take it David's not happy with you dating Pearce?"

Nanna wrapped her arms around herself, frowning. "Pearce hasn't always been the straightest arrow in the quiver." She smiled, surprising Flo.

"David's worried about how it will look for his campaign manager to be dating someone who..." Flo chose her words carefully. "...tests legal boundaries."

"Yes."

"You can't blame him, Nanna. He's a young mayor, picking his way carefully through dangerous political waters. If something blows up, he'll be dealing with it on both a personal and a professional level."

She sighed, scrubbing a hand over her eyes. "I know."

"Is it really worth it?"

Nanna seemed to consider Flo's question for a moment. She finally nodded. "For me, it is. I'm tired of playing it safe, Flo. I'm ready to spread my wings a little. Pearce is exciting. He's brutally honest and refreshingly straightforward. I never doubt where I stand with him. And he respects me as a strong, professional woman."

Flo barely kept surprise off her face. Were they talking about a different man? Everything she'd heard about Pearce to that point painted him as a womanizer. Not exactly someone who respected women in any capacity. Although, he could just be very good at presenting the image that each of his conquests wanted to see.

"Just be careful, Nanna," Flo said.

Nanna reached out and squeezed Flo's hand. Her fingers were icy and her grip was strong, almost desperate. "I was with Pearce in Indianapolis the night that unfortunate young woman was killed. He didn't kill her, Flo. I'll vouch for him."

Would she? Staring into Nanna's hopeful gaze, Flo wasn't sure if she saw truth there, or just a desperate need to believe. Just in case it was the latter, Flo said, "My friend Roger Attles is being looked at for the murder, Nanna. He's going to be arrested if I don't find the real killer. I can assure you that Roger didn't kill that poor woman. Which means if he's arrested, not only will an innocent man go to jail, but the real killer will still be on the streets."

To Flo's horror, Nanna's gaze slid away from hers, the green-brown depths colored with something that looked a little like guilt.

"I just want you to be aware of that as you're protecting your privacy," Flo said before turning away and heading back to Silver Hills.

CHAPTER ELEVEN

Flo had nearly bowed out several times. The idea of hopping around in a room filled with flailing limbs and energy just made her tired. She'd rather go try to talk to Mae's neighbors to see if anyone had seen or heard something that might shed light on Mae's murder.

She hesitated outside the activities room, her resolve warring with her sense of obligation.

"Flo!" several voices screamed at once.

She sighed, caught. Too late to escape.

TC gave her a grin and a little wave when she came into the room. The pretty brunette wore an orange tank top over lime green tights and looked cute as a bug with her long, dark hair pulled up in a high ponytail.

Agnes waved energetically to catch Flo's attention, as if she could have possibly missed her six-foot-tall friend in the room full of normal-heighted women.

Celia was doing stretches next to Agnes, her slim form looking spiffy in a short black t-shirt over a hot pink sport's bra and black capri leggings.

Agnes had on a loose-fitting white tee and black sweat pants that bunched just below her knees. She had a ratty white towel draped around the back of her neck. Her gray eyes sparkled with anticipation.

Flo couldn't help smiling back. "You look ready."

Agnes nodded, frowning at Flo's outfit. "You're going to roast in that long-sleeved shirt."

"I'll be fine. I'm not going to jump around a lot."

Celia and Agnes shared a chuckle.

Flo frowned. What did they know that they weren't telling her? "It's just dancing, right?"

Their laughter was cut short by TC calling out for everyone to take a last sip of water before they got started.

Flo grabbed her bottle of water and sipped, thinking she wouldn't really need it. Despite her earlier misgivings, the collective anticipation of the dozen or so women in the room was infectious and she took her place next to Agnes as TC headed over to her boom box.

"Okay, ladies, follow my movements. We'll go for ten-minute continuous spurts and then stop for a water and rest break. And remember, don't stress the dance moves, just keep moving and have fun."

TC hit a button on her boom box and a rich, heart-pounding Latin beat filled the room. Turning her back to the class, TC stood with her hands down, hips moving to the enticing rhythm.

Flo glanced around at the other women and saw a wide variety of skills and comfort levels, from stiff and jerky to smoothly swaying and loose-limbed.

Celia closed her eyes and gave herself up to the beat, her shoulders swaying with her hips. Agnes, despite her size, also looked comfortable swaying her hips to the rhythm.

Flo took a deep breath and pushed doubt aside, falling back on years of ballroom dancing classes to ease some of the stiffness from her moves.

The beat picked up and TC started to move, calling out instructions as she settled into the groove.

"Step, step, fist pump, sway the hips. Switch, step, step, pump, sway..."

Flo struggled to keep up with the rapid changes. She forced herself to tune out the manic movements next to her as Agnes launched herself into the dance.

"Fast steps for four, punch, punch, sway right, sway left, hop, hop, hop..."

Flo tripped over her own feet, her breath heaving in her throat. Sweat was already coating her face and her heart pounded as she struggled to keep up.

A sudden gust of air bathed her skin and her eyes went wide as a large fist shot past her nose, barely missing her face.

Flo's gaze shot to Agnes, who seemed to have forgotten all about TC and the class and had gone into her own routine, her strong, well-padded form swaying, swinging and hopping all over the place. Agnes' arms flailed, her legs swung wide, then narrow, then she planted hard, the floor creaking beneath her, and swung her hips wide.

One fleshy hip smacked into Flo and sent her stumbling sideways.

Celia gave a yelp as Agnes' hips made the return trip and connected with her slight form, launching her askew to bump into the woman dancing next to her.

Both women went down in a clumsy heap.

Agnes danced on, her face flushed, her eyes filled with the joy of the dance, and her steps becoming ever more energetic as the music swelled, the beat throbbing through the space.

At the front of the room, TC was just as immersed in the dance, her lithe form swaying, lean limbs taking the energetic steps with ease, long arms grasping the air as she performed a complex array of moves that involved every inch of her long body.

Flo took up a new spot a yard farther away from Agnes and refocused.

After several missteps and some serious timing issues, Flo finally picked up the choreography of the dance.

"Step forward, four steps, Ladies! Pump those fists. Little hip here. Walk it back..."

Flo expelled a frustrated breath. She'd just gotten the hang of the last set of moves. She did her best to follow TC's movements, feeling proud when she finally got it.

A blur of motion pulled her attention from the front of the room and she turned with a small cry as Agnes spun wildly in her direction, arms spread and fingers clutching the air.

Flo ran from the swinging arms and thought she'd escaped, when a thick leg swung out and clipped her behind her knees. She went down with a short bark of surprise, banging her knees on the hardwood floor

Dancers all around Agnes went down like dominos, either stumbling over their own feet trying to get away or mowed down by Agnes's swinging hips or flailing limbs.

Agnes didn't seem to notice. Her eyes were closed and she wore a perpetual smile on her face, her expression filled with joy.

"Quick steps here, tap forward, tap back, swing the arms in a wave, turn and other side..."

Celia tried to stand and had to duck almost immediately as Agnes whipped her arms overhead in a whirling motion, before launching herself to the right, hips swaying and then, as people scrambled wildly out of the way, in the other direction.

She was heading right for Flo, body in constant circular motion and feet slamming hard onto the floor as she performed a series of hopping, pointing, and swinging motions with her legs.

The music pulsed and throbbed.

The beat built.

Energy pulsed through the room.

Screams filled the air.

"Bend your legs, Ladies, on your toes, hop from left to right, right to left, arms swaying overhead..."

Agnes made like an Egyptian, her own version of TC's example more energetic by far than it ever needed to be.

All around her people cringed, pulled farther away, and shared looks of disbelief.

"Okay, Ladies," TC said. "Freestyle!"

All eyes went round. Several women glanced toward the door as if thinking about trying to escape. They must have realized they'd never make it. It was too far and the Zumba-drugged Tasmanian Devil known as Agnes was between them and the door.

The intensity of the music swelled. Energy pulsed.

Agnes wheeled, dipped, hopped, and flailed.

Flo reared back as a fist snapped toward her face.

Celia jumped sideways as a muscular leg swerved fast and hard toward her thigh.

Agnes let her head fall back, her eyes still closed, and shimmied her shoulders. Her knees bent, she threw her weight from side to side, hips pumping almost obscenely as she shimmied everything she had like a belly dancer on speed.

She came out of the crouch like a bullet shot from a gun, flinging herself to the right and swinging one arm up, one arm down.

Celia yelped and went down trying to avoid being punched.

Agnes whirled, performing the same maneuver to the front.

A forty-something woman from the single side hit the ground, crab-walking backward to avoid Agnes' thrashing feet.

Agnes whirled again, her big body in a full shimmy, hips whipping, breasts bouncing hard enough to dislocate somebody's nose, and totally oblivious to everything but the music as she did a step, slide, step, slide, arm-swing maneuver, heading right for Flo.

Flo fixed a scowl onto her face. She was *not* going down again. She growled in her throat, embracing her inner tiger, and stood her ground.

The last note hit the air, leaving behind a startling silence.

Agnes didn't stop with the music. She did one last step slide and flung her right arm up, her fist heading right for Flo's chin.

Flo's growl deepened. She blocked Agnes' upward strike with a downward strike of her own forearm and, reaching out as Agnes' eyes snapped open in surprise, flicked her friend hard between the eyes.

Agnes frowned, reaching up to rub her head. "Ow! Why'd you do that, Flo?"

"Because you're a menace," somebody mumbled behind Flo.

Dabbing her face with a towel, TC turned around, her pretty face filled with pleasure and glistening with sweat. Her grin slid slowly away when she saw the carnage Agnes had left in her wake.

Bodies were strewn everywhere. Women rubbing red places on their limbs, carefully pushed to their feet, favoring tender joints. Groans filled the air.

Agnes stood at the epicenter of it all. Her own brand of Level 5 hurricane.

Hurricane Agnes.

"What happened?" TC asked, all the joy of the dance seeping out of her. She hurried to help a woman whom Flo thought looked slightly familiar up off the floor.

"*Agnes* happened," Celia said, rubbing one of her hips.

"Hurricane Agnes," Flo said, feeling a grin tugging at her lips.

Agnes looked around, her eyes going wide. "Did I do that?"

"O-blivious," the woman standing next to TC said.

Then someone laughed.

Someone else joined in.

A hoot burst out of Celia's mouth and she gave into it, doubling over with laughter and holding her sides.

Flo felt a chuckle tickling her throat and set it free, reaching to give a sweaty, panting Agnes a hug. "I have to say, hun. With you around, nothing is ever boring."

Agnes gave her a wincing smile, glancing around as, one by one, the other dancers joined in the laughter. Then she shrugged and reached for her water bottle. "That was fun."

The room erupted in howls and hoots.

AS WOMEN DRIFTED FROM the room, sweaty and happily chatting, TC motioned for Flo to join her and the woman she'd helped from the floor.

TC put an arm around the other woman's shoulders and smiled. "Flo, this is Renee Woldigger."

"Hi Renee," Flo said. "It's so nice to meet you."

Renee eyed Flo for a beat before taking her hand in a limp, slightly sweaty grip. "Flo. How are you?" Her light-brown gaze skimmed toward TC, looking confused.

TC hurried to explain. "Flo's looking into poor Mae Caldone's death."

Renee's eyes widened. When she nodded, the extra flesh beneath her pointy chin wobbled. "Elisa told me about that. So sad."

"Yes. Elisa said you overheard Mae talking to someone in the gym here at Silver Hills?" Flo prompted.

Renee's head bobbed as she warmed to the purpose of the conversation. She shoved frizzy brown hair behind one ear, leaning closer to Flo as if she was about to share a secret. "It was a man. And they didn't seem happy with each other, either. They kept their voices low but their body language was stiff."

"Could you hear what they were talking about?" TC asked.

"Only a few words here and there. The gist of it was that Mae thought he was bothering her and she wanted him to leave her alone. He was rude about it, too. He told her to keep her mouth shut." Renee crossed her arms over her narrow chest. "I don't like men who think so little of women that they don't let them have an opinion on things." She shook her head, her brows lowering over the stormy brown gaze.

"What did the man look like?" Flo asked, her fingers twining nervously together.

"I didn't get a really good look at him," Renee said. They were standing in the back corner of the room, near all the weight-lifting equipment. His face was obscured by a piece of equipment and he wore a ball cap over his hair."

"Is there anything you can tell me about him?" Flo asked, feeling frustration build as she realized her hopes for identifying their killer were sliding away.

"He was tall and lean. I remember thinking he was dressed too well to be at the gym."

"What do you mean, too well?" TC asked.

"Black slacks, like a businessman would wear. And a light gray button-down shirt. I did notice he was wearing shiny black shoes."

"You didn't get an impression of age, then?" Flo tried in desperation.

Renee's head bobbed. "I'm really good with ages. I'm almost certain he was in his mid to late forties."

Flo wished she could grab onto that and run with it. But, realistically, it meant less than nothing since Renee hadn't gotten a good look at the man and general impressions from a distance with obstacles obscuring the view were not conducive to accurate eye-witness reports.

Flo had learned that and much more during her hours working at the Silver City Police Department as a part-time filing clerk in the evidence dungeon.

"Okay. Thanks for your help, Renee. If you think of anything else, will you tell me?" Flo handed the other woman a card.

"Of course," Renee nodded, the bags under her eyes wiggling. "It's very exciting to be a key witness in a murder investigation."

CHAPTER TWELVE

"What's next on the docket?" Agnes asked. She punched the button on the elevator and Flo stepped inside, too tired to even use the steps to go down one level to her apartment.

"Don't you have a date with Hertz tonight?"

Agnes winced, shaking her head. "No. I told him I was busy."

Something was definitely going on there and Flo would give her left molar to know what it was. "Do you want to talk about it?"

"Nope." Agnes held a hand over the face of the door to keep it from closing.

"Okay, well, I was going to have dinner at Le Petit Bistro. I'd like to talk to François about Pearce."

Agnes grinned. "I can do dinner."

"Good. I'll meet you at the front doors at five. Hopefully we'll beat the crowds."

"See you there."

The elevator doors slid shut and Flo was left to rehash everything she knew by herself. The prospect didn't thrill her as it usually did. It seemed everywhere she turned was bad news.

News that seemed to be pointing toward a certain kind, handsome lawyer she was trying to save.

Her cell rang as she was stepping off the elevator. Speak of the devil. "Roger! How are you feeling?" she asked in lieu of a greeting.

"Hey, doll. Other than a persistent dull throb behind my eyes I'm right as rain. I just wanted to let you know there's no need to come visit me tonight. Richard's working on springing me now."

Guilt slipped through her. Flo had been too busy plotting her next move in the investigation to think about visiting Roger. "That's really good news." She had an idea. "Are you up to a small outing? Agnes and I are having dinner at Le Petit Bistro. Would you and Richard like to join us?"

"I'll ask him. What time are you going?"

"We'll get there a little after five. I was going to ask the owner about Mae."

Silence filled the line. Flo inserted her key, the sound of Rodney's nails clacking on the tile of the entry making her smile.

"Do you have reason to believe he's involved?" Roger sounded wary and Flo couldn't help wondering why.

"Not of her murder, no. But someone told me Pearce had been hanging around François' restaurants, both in Indy and here. That makes me wonder what their relationship is."

"You're thinking Pearce killed Mae?"

"He's definitely a strong suspect." Something in the tone of Roger's voice made her ask, "Do you disagree?"

"I don't know, doll. If he'd killed her himself, why would he go out of his way to come here and accuse me of it?"

"Obviously, he's trying to pin it on you. If he did it, you being blamed for the murder would be the best thing that could happen as far as Pearce was concerned. From everything I've learned about Nicholai Pearce, he's devious and determined. If he thought blaming you would take the heat off himself, I believe he'd do it in a heartbeat."

"I guess." Roger didn't sound convinced.

"It doesn't hurt to take a look at him, right? I don't have a lot of prospects." And like it or not, Roger was one of the few.

"Not at all. You're right. I'm just..." He sighed. "I'm not feeling much like a battle right now."

"Fortunately, you don't need to fight this one. You have me, Agnes, and TC to do it for you." Flo tried to make her tone light, hoping to make him smile.

He did her one better. Roger chuckled. "That's the best team a man could ask for. Just be careful, doll. Somebody's already killed once. They're not going to think twice about doing it again."

"Believe me, I know it. We're simply asking questions. If we find out anything that implicates a killer, I'll go to Detective Peters with it."

"Promise?"

"Girl scouts honor."

He chuckled again. "Here's Richard. We'll meet you at the restaurant at five-ish. I'm looking forward to it."

FLO AND AGNES ARRIVED at Le Petit Bistro a few minutes before five. They stood at the podium in front of the door and looked around at the bustling restaurant.

"It's a good thing you got us reservations," Agnes said. "This place is hopping again."

"I guess the novelty hasn't worn off," Flo agreed.

The hostess was a different woman than the one who'd seated them before. The elegant woman with beautiful dark hair swept into a tidy chignon came over to them, smiling widely. "Welcome to Le Petit Bistro. Two for dinner?"

Flo shook her head. "I had a reservation for four under the name Bee."

The woman's snug black dress swished as she moved behind the podium and examined a computer screen. "There it is! I have a table for you in front of the garden window. If you'll follow me?"

They fell in behind the woman and wove between the diners to a pretty table covered in a red and white checkered cloth. A flickering candle sent waves of golden light over a small vase filled with a single, long-stemmed red rose surrounded by baby's breath.

"Will this do?" the woman asked, her dark gaze widening with the question.

"It's perfect, thank you so much," Flo answered.

They sat and the hostess settled menus in front of them. "I highly recommend the French onion soup. It's a specialty of the house."

Before the woman could leave, Flo stopped her. "I was hoping to talk to François. Is he here tonight?"

"I believe he left early. Family obligations. Is there something I can help you with?"

Flo let her disappointment show. "I doubt you can. I wanted to ask him about someone who's frequented both his Indy restaurant and this one."

The woman clasped her hands in front of her, resting them on her slightly rounded belly. "I've worked for François for two decades. First as his hostess at La Délicatesse and now here. I might be able to help."

Flo reached into her purse and pulled out a card. "I'm helping the police look into the murder of a young woman. I understand a person of interest in the investigation might have been a regular customer at both restaurants. I thought maybe François might be able to tell me about the man."

The woman examined the card, her lips tightening. "You're speaking of Mr. Pearce."

Flo fought to hide the spike of excitement. "Yes. You know him?"

"Not personally. But I'm aware of him. He's caused no end of trouble for poor François."

"How so?"

The woman glanced around and, after a moment, sat in an empty chair and leaned close so she could lower her voice. "He used to show up nearly every weekend night and ask François to consider making him a partner. When François refused, Pearce would ask for a table and then proceed to complain about the food and service and loudly bad mouth the chef." She shook her head. "He cost us many a skilled server with his antics. Several girls fled crying from his brutal treatment."

"Why didn't you just refuse to serve him?" Agnes asked.

"We tried. He caused a terrible scene, even going so far as to accuse the restaurant of trying to cover up food poisoning incidents and roach infestations." She sighed. "He was the bane of our existence. I'm more than half convinced Mr. Pearce was the reason François decided to pick up his family and move down here to Silver City."

"And here he is again," Flo said, giving the woman a sympathetic glance.

"Yes." The hostess shook her head. "I just can't believe he moved down here. But then he always did have an eye for Sophie. Not that she would every reciprocate. She loves François to distraction."

"Has Mr. Pearce repeated his harassment at Le Petite Bistro?"

"Not yet. But he's here all the time, staring at François as if to intimidate him. Poor François is at his wit's end. And seeing him meet the Mayor here..." She shook her head. "It seemed too much like a power play. Between you and me, I think it might have been the last straw." The hostess looked around at the bustling restaurant, her expression sad. "He's talking about closing both places down. He's beyond frustrated at this point."

"That would be a shame," Flo said.

They sat in silence for a beat and then the woman placed her hands on the tabletop. "I should get back to work."

Flo held her gaze as she stood. "I'm going to help," she promised. "There has to be something that can be done about Pearce."

The hostess nodded, frowned, and walked away. She didn't look like she believed Flo would be able to help.

A moment later the front door opened and Roger came in. He looked around and Agnes waved energetically to catch his eye. He hurried over, wincing slightly as he approached the table. A stark white bandage showed through his gray hair at the back of his head. "Good evening, ladies." Roger bent down and kissed Flo on the cheek. His lips held the chill of the frigid night beyond the windows. He eased slowly into a chair, wincing again.

"Does your head still hurt?" Flo asked, giving his hand a squeeze.

"Like the dickens. But I just took my pain medications. It should feel better in a bit."

"Where's Richard," Agnes asked, looking hopefully toward the door. She'd had half a crush on the day manager at Silver Hills since she'd moved into the place. Unfortunately, Richard Attles didn't feel the same way about her.

"He couldn't join us. He has to go spell the vamps. I told him you'd give me a ride home."

"Of course," Flo said, favoring Agnes with a smile when her friend looked disappointed.

A young man in a pristine white shirt and black slacks showed up with a pad, smiling around the table. "Hello. I'm Adulf. I'll be meeting your gastronomic needs tonight. Can I get a drink order?"

Flo ordered wine and Agnes ordered her usual beer. Roger stuck to water.

"It's probably not a good idea to mix wine with my pain meds," he told them after Adulf had hurried away to get their drinks. "How has your day been going?" he asked with his usual genuine interest.

Flo and Agnes told him about Zumba and Flo was pleased to see him laughing along with them. By the time they were done with the subject, Adulf had returned.

Roger ordered the recommended soup, claiming lack of appetite. Flo and Agnes both got chicken marsala and Caesar salads. When the waiter had left to put their orders in, Flo filled Roger in on what the hostess had said about Pearce.

He started frowning early in the story and his frown only deepened as it progressed. "The man's a cad."

"Yes, he is. On so many levels," Flo agreed.

She turned to Agnes, realizing her friend had been very quiet. Every time they discussed Nicholai Pearce, Agnes went uncharacteristically quiet.

"You're not saying much," she prompted her friend. "Have you met our newest resident?"

Agnes shook her head, stuffing a heavily buttered chunk of French bread into her mouth and chewing slowly.

Flo recognized evasion tactics when she saw them. She arched a brow at Agnes.

When her friend started to speak with her mouth still full, Flo held up a finger.

Agnes finally swallowed, frowning at Flo. "What?"

"What aren't you telling me?" Then a thought occurred and she didn't like it. "Pearce hasn't hurt you, has he?"

Agnes snorted out a laugh, spitting a chunk of French bread in Flo's direction. "Hurt me? He wouldn't dare."

Agnes was a strong woman. Normally, Flo wouldn't even consider her a victim. But Pearce did seem to create hard feelings wherever he went. "Talk to me. Something's bothering you."

Agnes shook her head but her gaze skimmed to Roger as if his presence was constraining her.

Roger took the hint. "I'm going to run to the little boy's room."

When he was halfway across the room, Agnes said. "It's not me. It's Hertz. Apparently, he had some deal with Pearce when they were both living in Indianapolis. They did some kind of business together."

"What's dire about that?" Flo asked, not understanding.

Agnes buttered another chunk of bread. "Hertz won't talk about it. But ever since Pearce moved into Silver Hills, Hertz just wants to move out." Agnes glanced toward the short hallway were the restrooms were. "Don't tell Roger. Hertz would be devastated if Roger was disappointed in him."

"Why would Roger be disappointed?"

Agnes shrugged but wouldn't give her any more details. Either she truly didn't have details, or she just wasn't comfortable divulging Hertz's business. By the time Roger returned, Flo realized she was going to have to go to the source. It was high time she and Hertz Thomson had a good talk.

CHAPTER THIRTEEN

François emerged from the back of the restaurant as they were getting ready to leave. Flo put a hand on Roger's arm when she saw him. "Can you wait a minute? I'd like to speak to the owner for a minute."

Roger nodded, indicating the table. "Agnes and I will order another drink."

"Thank you." Flo hurried toward François, noting the way his expression changed when he saw her coming. His gaze shifted toward the hallway, and Flo saw the moment he thought about turning around and leaving.

But, instead, he pushed the corners of his lips up into a smile. "Bonjour, Mrs. Bee, is it?" He took her hand. "It's so nice to see you again."

"I was wondering if you could give me a couple minutes of your time."

He glanced at his watch, not even seeming to see it before shaking his head. "I'm so sorry. I'm in a bit of a rush tonight."

"I promise it won't take long."

Frown lines marred his smooth forehead, but he nodded. "In my office?"

"That would be fine."

She followed him past the restrooms to an unmarked door near the exit at the back of the restaurant. He opened the door and shoved it inward, motioning for Flo to precede him into the cramped space.

He hurried in after her, grabbing a stack of cookbooks off the extra chair. "I apologize for the mess. It's always a bit wild around the holidays."

Flo thanked him and sat in the newly cleared chair, the hard seat almost as unforgiving as the cookbooks would have been. She sat back and the legs creaked ominously. Forcing a smile, Flo joked, "Maybe I shouldn't have let Agnes talk me into the Creme Brulee."

François chuckled, dropping wearily into the chair behind his age-pocked wood desk. "What can I help you with, Mrs. Bee?" Before she could respond, his expression tightened with worry. "You didn't have a bad food experience?"

"No. Nothing like that."

"Service?"

"Perfect. No complaints."

He relaxed, sitting back in his chair. "*Bien*. As you can imagine, starting a new place has been a bit of a challenge."

"Business has certainly been good. Whatever problems you've had, it seems you've managed to keep it under wraps."

"I'm lucky that a few of my key employees were willing to relocate."

"I met your hostess earlier. She's wonderful."

His smile was tight. "*Oui*. Bethany is an invaluable employee and friend." He lifted his arms, glancing around. "None of this would have happened without her. She's always loved Silver City. Her mother lives here."

"I told her I wanted to speak with you and she mentioned you were gone for the night."

"Yes. I'd intended to be. I forgot something and..." He sighed. "I'm afraid I'm having trouble balancing work and family right now. I feel a bit as if the restaurant will collapse if I don't keep an eagle eye on it."

"I certainly understand that," Flo told him. "I can't imagine all the moving parts in an operation like this."

He nodded. "So...?"

"I'm sorry for keeping you. I wondered if you could tell me what you know about Nicholai Pearce?"

François looked confused. "Pearce? I...he's eaten here several times since we opened."

As responses went, Flo gave it a C-. He hadn't overtly lied, but he'd left out enough information to fill a novel. "You'd never met him before moving to Silver City?"

He eyed her carefully, no doubt trying to decide if she already knew the answer to her question. She would have been stupid to ask a question for which she didn't already know the correct response, but Flo had no idea if the man sitting across from her thought she was stupid or not.

Apparently, he had a high enough opinion of her. He sighed. "I *have*, actually. He used to come into La Délicatesse. I'll admit I was surprised to see him here, but then the two cities aren't really all that far apart. Many people commute into Indy from the southern Indiana towns."

"How well do you know Mr. Pearce," she asked.

François shrugged. "Not well. I've spoken to him briefly a handful of times. He's obviously a good customer, I try to introduce myself to the regulars."

"What did you think of him?"

"He seems like a nice enough guy." François held her gaze, his expression carefully neutral.

He was lying to her about Pearce. "Your hostess mentioned that Nicholai Pearce was interested in engaging a partnership with you."

She left it there, letting him pick through her abrupt statement and figure out what she was thinking. Would he realize she knew he was lying?

"He did suggest a few times that he'd like to invest in the restaurant. I thanked him politely but declined. I prefer to keep full control of my investments."

"And he didn't cause a fuss over your refusal?"

"Not at all. He was persistent but cordial."

Well, someone was certainly lying. Either François or Bethany. Flo wondered which of the two might have a reason to lie. François might simply be trying to avoid airing his dirty laundry. Bethany, she supposed, could have been spurned by Pearce. He seemed to leave broken romances in his wake like a Love Boat type cruise ship.

Flo didn't want to get Bethany in trouble, so she decided to try another tack. "Do you know a woman named Mae Caldone?"

He frowned. "Isn't that the woman who was killed?"

"Yes. She lived at Silver Hills, on the singles side."

"You live there too?" François asked, his handsome face filled with horror.

"I do. It's been quite a shock."

He shook his head. "I can imagine. But why would you ask me about her? And why all the questions about Mr. Pearce?"

"She was in a relationship with Nicholai Pearce. She'd told more than one person that someone was being aggressive with her in the days before her murder. I actually witnessed her fighting with Mr. Pearce outside this restaurant. And I know she'd been a customer here," Flo said, thinking about the receipts she'd seen in Mae's apartment. "I just wondered if you'd seen them here together?"

"I don't believe I have. I saw a picture of the woman on the news after her death. She didn't look at all familiar to me."

"I'm sorry. I have to ask..."

"Where was I on the night she was murdered?" He laughed sadly. "When was it?"

"Saturday evening. Between five and eight pm."

"I would have been here. In the restaurant. That's our busiest time of the day and day of the week. Bethany can verify my alibi." He shook his head, frowning slightly. "I never dreamed I'd ever need an alibi for a murder. It's a bit disconcerting."

A soft knock sounded on the door and it opened. A small, light-haired woman stuck her head through, her smile drooping as she spotted Flo. "Oh, I'm so soree," she said in a soft, accented voice. "I will come back."

François stood abruptly. "No, *chérie*. Come in. Mrs. Bee was just leaving."

Flo stood as François wrapped an arm around the slender woman, who managed to make a fitted white button-down shirt over slim denim capris look elegant. "Sophie, this is Mrs. Bee. She's helping the police find out who killed that poor woman from the news. Mrs. Bee, my beautiful wife, Sophia."

Flo took the other woman's hand, finding it soft and carefully manicured. "It's a pleasure."

Sophia Liberte's pale cheeks flushed. "The pleasure ese all mine, Mrs. Bee." She frowned. "What do we know of theze woman's death?"

"Nothing, *chérie*," François told his wife. "Mrs. Bee thought maybe she'd eaten here with Monsieur Pearce, that's all."

The couple shared a look that seemed filled with meaning. Sophia's cheeks flushed a deeper pink. "Oh, I see."

Her cornflower blue gaze looked even brighter lined at top and bottom with thick lines of black eyeliner. Watching her, Flo couldn't help thinking that Sophia Liberte wanted to say something more, but her husband moved around her and opened the door, clearly asking Flo to leave.

"It was so nice meeting you," Flo said as she stepped into the hallway.

The door closed and Flo turned to find a young woman, probably in her early teens, leaning against the paneled wall with a bored look on her pretty face. Her eyes were the same shade of blue as her mother's and her long, black hair was curled at the ends like Sophia's hair. But her tall, lanky form more resembled François'. "Hello," Flo said, giving the girl a friendly smile.

The girl's eyes narrowed briefly and she mumbled a quick, embarrassed, "hello," before sticking her face in her phone again, dismissing Flo as easily as her father had.

"FRANÇOIS' WIFE KNOWS something about Pearce she's not telling," Flo told Agnes later as they sat in the Silver Hills bar drinking wine. Or, in Agnes' case, a very large beer.

"Why do you say that?" Celia asked.

"I sensed that she wanted to tell me something. But François cut her off and hurried me out of there. How well do you know Sophia Liberte?" Flo asked her friend.

"Not all that well. As I said, we've had dinner with them a couple of times. The kids are darling."

Flo noticed that Celia always seemed to talk about the kids when she asked about Sophia and she pointed it out.

Celia flushed. "Really? I hadn't even realized I was doing that." She frowned. "Maybe it's because Sophia is such a wall-flower. She has no real identity of her own. She definitely lives in the shadow of her husband and kids."

"Well, that shadow is keeping her from telling me something that might be helpful," Flo said.

"Then we need to bring her into the light," Agnes said, grinning.

Flo looked at Agnes and pointed to her own lips. "You have a foam mustache."

Undeterred, Agnes licked foam off her mouth. "I'm serious, Flo.

"I know. And I agree. We need to get her alone somehow."

"How are we going to do that?" Celia asked. "As far as I know, she never goes anywhere without either her kids or her husband. Except for having lunch once a week at Le Petite Bistro and being on a couple of boards, she's pretty much always at home."

"Can we approach her at home?" Flo asked.

"Not without François finding out about it. We'd need a good reason to be there."

Flo's imagination was already onto something. "What kinds of boards is Sophia on?"

Celia shrugged. "You know, the usual. The hospital, the parks, the PTA.

Why?" Agnes asked. "What are you thinking?"

"I'm thinking it's time to have another Christmas Festival of Lights planning meeting."

Frowning, Agnes shook her head. "We just had one, Flo. Our next one is scheduled for next week. Don't you read your emails?"

"I know that, Agnes!" Flo said, irritated. "I'm talking about an excuse to go to the Liberte home."

Celia's eyes widened as she caught Flo's drift. "To invite her to be on the planning committee." She nodded. "That's perfect. Sophia's a sucker for anything having to do with children and she'll want to donate to the toy drive." Celia nodded. "I like it."

"Do you know where they live?" Flo asked her friend.

Ce nodded. "I've been there once. They live in the Grandwood Estates."

Agnes made a face. "That's gated. Will we be able to get inside without somebody's help?"

"You leave that to me," Celia said with a smug smile. "I've got connections."

CHAPTER FOURTEEN

It was afternoon of the next day before they could put their plan into motion. Grandwood Estates was on the north end of Silver City. It included a dozen homes that were valued from the high one millions to close to three million dollars. It was old money, for the most part, and much of it had been transplanted from Indianapolis. What the community lacked in neighborly welcome, due to the gated entrance, ten-acre lots and the long, winding drives peppered with "No Trespassing" signs, it more than made up for in haughty self-importance.

But Flo tried not to judge the people living there too harshly. Some of their best donors for the Festival of Lights and their annual Thanksgiving food drive lived in Grandwood.

"I thought Ce would be here by now," Flo said, casting a glance around the area.

"She'll be here," Agnes said with a little too much certainty.

Flo narrowed her gaze at the woman in the passenger seat. She'd seen Celia and Agnes with their heads together in the lobby at Silver Hills before they'd left. Soon afterward, Celia declared she'd have to meet them at Grandwood. She had an errand she needed to run first.

"What have you two cooked up?" Flo asked Agnes.

One thing about Agnes was that she was a terrible liar. "I don't know what you're talking about, Flo." Her gaze skimmed quickly away, landing on the rear-view mirror.

The man who came out of the little guard building next to the gate was built like a linebacker and had the scarred face and crooked nose of a gangster. He wore a heavy dark-blue jacket over matching blue pants. The guard glared at Flo as she drove up to the closed metal gate. He rested a hand on his weapon as if he thought he might have to fight his way out of a geriatric shootout.

She rolled down her window and smiled up at him. "Hello. We're here to see Mrs. Liberte."

The guard leaned down and peered past Flo to Agnes, his gaze going hard. "Names."

"Florence Bee and Agnes Willard," Flo told him in her most harmless-sounding voice.

"I'll check the approved visitor list. But I'm pretty sure you're not on it," he said. The man skimmed his hostile glare over them one more time, as if hoping to intimidate them away from visiting, and then straightened, turning toward the gate-house.

Behind them, tires squealed and a short scream filled the air.

The guard whipped around as a large SUV careened around the corner and wobbled toward them, its big nose heading straight for Flo's car.

All Flo could see beyond the windshield was a pair of wild blue eyes and a ratty mop of blonde hair.

Seconds before it would have struck them, the big car jerked sideways and hit the grass, its oversized tires digging tracks in the lush carpet of green before crashing into the big evergreens that dotted the green space.

Flo grabbed her door handle and wrenched it open as Agnes climbed out of the car. She turned to the SUV, frowning as the woman inside screamed like her hair was on fire.

She was vaguely aware of Agnes running around the front of the car as she took a step, fully intending to go see what she could do to help.

A mechanism groaned softly behind her. Flo turned to see the gate slowly creaking open.

Agnes ran past again. "Get in the car, Flo."

Flo frowned, her gaze sliding from the gate to the distraught woman, who was screaming something about her legs, her hands pummeling the guard's arms and chest as if she was hysterical.

Agnes slammed her door. "Come *on*, Flo!"

The guard tried to open the door of the SUV and the woman shrieked, throwing her head back and screaming, "My legs! My legs!"

Flo hesitated another moment. "That voice is familiar..."

"Flo!" She turned to find Agnes leaning across the seat, her gaze wide with alarm. "Come *on*!"

The guard leaned into the SUV's driver side window and the woman's face appeared around his shoulder. One, elegant hand swept out the window and motioned toward the gate.

"Is that...?"

"Flo!"

She wrenched her gaze away from the nightmare in the trees and hurried back to the car, sliding quickly inside and driving through the gate to the sound of more screaming.

A moment later, they pulled up to the address Celia had given them and she slammed the car into *Park*, turning to glare at Agnes. "You could have told me."

Agnes grinned. "Celia was afraid you wouldn't go for it."

Shaking her head, Flo sighed. They were right. She wouldn't have.

"Mass tried to get us inside but he found out the Liberte's don't see any visitors at their home. We were going to be turned away if we didn't do something tricky."

How sad for them that they didn't feel safe inviting people into their home, Flo couldn't help thinking. Then she grinned. But as long as she lived, she'd never get over the sight of Celia in full-throated distraction mode. "Mass is going to kill her for scratching up his SUV."

Agnes shrugged. "He can afford to get it fixed."

THE FRONT DOOR OPENED before they even reached it. Sophia Liberte frowned prettily as if trying to remember who they were. She gave them a kind smile. "Hello. Can I help you?"

Flo offered her hand. "Florence Bee. We met at Le Petite Bistro?"

The other woman's expression cleared. "Ah, yes. Mrs. Bee. It's so nice to see you again."

Despite the words, Sophia looked less than pleased. Her pretty blue gaze was wary as she looked to Agnes. She glanced once toward the gate in the distance, no doubt wondering how they'd managed to get past the guard.

"This is my friend, Agnes Willard." Flo said, attempting to distract her from that line of thought. "We're friends of Celia Angonetti's."

"Celia?" The smile became more genuine. An awkward silence fell between them and then, rather reluctantly Flo thought, Sophia stepped back, opening the door wider. "Please, come inside. It's bitter out there today."

"Thank you. We're sorry to just drop in on you like this. We're in the beginning stages of planning for our Christmas Festival of Lights at Silver Hills and...well..." Flo gave the other woman an embarrassed smile. "I'm afraid we lost one of our committee members recently. Celia thought you might be willing to step in and help."

Pure delight filled Sophia's face. Flo almost felt badly that the invitation was a ruse. The younger woman clapped her hands. "How lovely! I've heard about your festival of lights. It's very popular here in Silver City. I would definitely like to hear more."

Flo nodded. "Good. Shall we sit down and chat?"

"Oh my! What terrible manners I have. Yes. Please come." She motioned for them to follow her into a large living area with pristine white leather couches facing off in front of a large, white-marble-fronted fireplace. A hearty fire danced prettily in the gas fireplace, giving the room a warmth that felt good to Flo after the outside temps.

Winter was definitely on its way to Silver City.

"Sit wherever you'd like. Can I get you tea?"

As tempting as that sounded, Flo said no, giving Agnes a look to keep her from asking for cookies too.

After glaring at Flo, Agnes dropped gracelessly onto one of the couches. "You have a beautiful home," she told Sophia.

Their hostess looked around as if she hadn't noticed and then smiled. "It is lovely. We're really happy here." The words lacked a genuine feel, as if Sophia said them a lot but never really thought about what they meant.

"Do the kids like their school?"

"They do," she nodded. "Well, my daughter is fifteen and my son is twelve. Difficult ages. So, who knows if they really like anything?" Her laughter rang a bit false and Flo read the worry in her expression.

"I'm so glad to have run into you at the restaurant yesterday. It's a wonderful place. Your husband's done a great job with it."

Sophia nodded but didn't comment. If anything, she held herself a bit stiffly as she lowered gracefully onto the opposite couch and crossed her slender legs.

There was some tension there, though Flo could only guess what it might be. François had seemed very loving with Sophia, protective. "Was it hard moving out of Indy?"

Only the barest hesitation gave Sophia away. But her answering smile was wide. If Flo hadn't been comparing the bright curve of lips to the woman's eyes, she might have believed it. "Not at all. It's a huge relief being away from all that traffic. The violence." She shuddered.

"But I'll bet you left friends behind," Flo nudged.

"I did. Several really good ones." Her smiled dimmed. "But Robert and Angie recommended me for the advisory board of the museum so I'll be visiting them often." Her expression showed true pleasure at the thought.

Flo nodded, wondering how she could broach the subject of Nicholai Pearce if Sophia didn't bring it up. Then she realized what Sophia had said. "Museum? Which museum?"

"I'm soree, I shouldn't have assumed you'd know Robert and Angie. My best friend, Angie is assistant curator at the Museum of Art. Robert is an archivist. They met on the job." She chuckled softly. "They love that place to pieces."

"Really? That's interesting. The man I was asking your husband about, Nicolai Pearce, was just at the Art Museum. In fact, he used it as his alibi for the murder of Mae Caldone."

Sophia blinked in surprise. "Oh." She shook her head. "I'm soree I cannot tell you more. I do not know him."

The woman's accent thickened suddenly, until she sounded very French. "Is it possible he knows your friends?"

"No." She shook her head with such determination, Flo wondered if she'd struck a nerve.

Her lips bending upward in a tight smile, Sophie said, "You wanted to talk to me about your Festival?"

Flo nodded, filling the other woman in on the requirements of joining the planning meeting and the goals of the event. "Many of the children in this area don't have much. We try to provide a good meal, a chance to visit with Santa, and a gift for as many children as our donors allow. If you don't think being active in the planning sounds like something you'd like to do, we'd be very grateful for any donation you could offer."

The planning committee had been a ruse to get them through Sophia Liberte's door. But talking about the event always brought out Flo's passion for what they were trying to accomplish with it. She didn't have to fake her enthusiasm.

"Of course I'd love to help in any way possible. We will certainly donate money and toys. But I'd be honored to help with the planning too. I was part of a similar event in Indianapolis. I might have some good ideas to offer."

"That would be wonderful." Flo stood and offered Sophia her hand. "Thank you so much for your time. I hope we haven't inconvenienced you too much."

Sophia stood too and clasped Flo's hand. Her grip was strong and sure. "Not at all. I'm glad you thought of me."

Agnes pointed to a picture on the wall. It was an enlarged photo of the Liberte's other restaurant. "That's beautiful. I've never eaten there."

Sophia stopped in front of the photo, her expression sad. "It was François' and my dream. When it became a success, we could hardly believe our luck."

Ownership. That was the expression on Sophia's attractive face. She felt a sense of ownership with La Délicatesse. Flo didn't think Sophia felt the same thing about Le Petite Bistro.

"You loved that restaurant, didn't you?" Flo asked. "I can see it in your face."

"Yes. I still help out there occasionally. It is a very special place."

Flo debated with herself for only a moment before she took a risk. "We heard that Nicholai Pearce was very disruptive there. I'm surprised you weren't aware."

Something flashed through the cornflower blue gaze. Something hard. Angry. When Sophia looked at Flo, her expression was no longer innocuous. "I don't focus on negative things, Mrs. Bee. That man is poison. He has nearly ruined our lives. I don't wish to think about him. Now, if that is all..."

They were being dismissed.

Flo inclined her head, feeling bad but not willing to let go of the larger issue. "I'm sorry. A woman has been killed. I'm just trying to find out who..."

"Please leave," Sophia interrupted.

Flo saw no way around it.

So they left.

"SOPHIA LIBERTE CERTAINLY seems to be a delicate flower," Agnes said on a grimace. Agnes thought of herself as a strong woman, both physically and mentally, and she believed women who seemed too delicate to survive life gave the gender a bad name.

Flo thought about what Agnes had said for a moment and then pulled over to the curb, putting the car into Park. After a moment she turned to Agnes. "Did her reaction seem a bit over the top to you? I mean, from what Bethany told me, Pearce was definitely a problem for the Libertes. But *ruined their lives*? That seems extreme to me." She frowned. "You don't suppose Pearce did something...personal to her, do you?" Flo didn't need to spell it out. Assault is something every woman thinks about when dealing with an aggressive man. But Flo really hoped she was off base with her suspicions.

"Probably not. The woman's big on drama for sure. But, I've met her type before. They love playing the victim. If she's surrounded by people who give her what she wants when she's victimized, she probably feeds on that validation."

Flo thought about what Agnes said, finally nodding. "You're right. She's probably just falling back on behavior that's benefitted her before." But Mae Caldone's story of Pearce's behavior, added to Bethany's accounts of his actions and Bonnie Feckle's experiences with the man gave Sophia's behavior additional weight.

What didn't make sense was Sophia's husband's statements about Pearce. Thinking of the vast differences, Flo murmured, "One of these things is not like the others." Flo's phone rang. She was surprised to see Nana Potts' name on the screen. "Nanna, how are you?"

"Flo. To tell you the truth, I've been better. Do you think you could come out to the house?"

Flo glanced at Agnes, widening her eyes. "Right now?"

"If you can?"

"Sure. Agnes is with me. We'll be there in a few minutes."

CHAPTER FIFTEEN

The Potts family's big stone ranch looked just as it had before, minus the fluttering of hundreds of hateful flyers around the end of their long drive and the body draped over the stump near the chicken coop.

As Flo climbed out of the car, the familiar stench of the distant chicken processing plant also reminded her that things hadn't changed much.

Dave Potts might be dead, but life at the Potts ranch went on.

Agnes' nose wrinkled under the smell. She covered her face, grimacing. "I'd have thought the smell would be better in cold weather."

Flo didn't respond. She was too curious what Nanna Potts wanted to talk to her about. Was she going to admit she'd lied about being Pearce's alibi?

Nanna answered the door after the first knock. Whether in fear for the state of her heavy wood doors under Agnes' less-than-gentle assault or because she'd been anxiously awaiting their arrival, Flo didn't know.

Judging by the woman's taut features and jerky movements, Flo could hazard a guess. "Are you all right, hun?" Flo asked as she stepped inside.

"No, she's not," a familiar deep voice said from the large room to their left.

A sense of déjà vu swept Flo as she watched the Potts son striding toward them. Except that the last time she'd been at the house, the son in question had been Peter Potts, the younger son.

Flo offered David Potts Junior a careful smile. "Mayor. I didn't realize you'd be here."

Nanna moved past them into the great room, pointing toward the long, lemon-yellow couch Flo remembered from her last visit. "Please, let's sit down," she said firmly, throwing her son a warning glare. "We'll have a calm and focused conversation." Her tone was more than suggestion. It was filled with the admonition her look promised.

Flo and Agnes moved into the room. Despite the cold temps outside, the sun formed long stripes on the rug-strewn hardwood floor, turning it bright and cheery. The wall of French doors that had looked out over a patio and a beautiful landscape of grass and trees before, currently framed a stark winter terrain of bare trees and browning grass.

They sat, everyone's gaze turning expectantly to the mayor.

He didn't hesitate to get to the point of their visit. "I've been threatened."

Flo blinked in surprise. She certainly hadn't been expecting that. "Threatened how?"

He reached into the pocket of his navy suit coat and pulled out a folded sheet of paper, handing it to Flo. "That was waiting for me when I got to my office today. It had been shoved under the locked door."

Flo carefully unfolded the piece of paper, using the edges as much as she could in case the police dusted it for prints. The page looked to have been created on a computer and printed in black and white. Across the top, in large letters, was a single sentence: "Unless you want this to get out to the press, you'll pay."

Flo's gaze slid past the title to the grainy black and white picture. The image was slightly unfocused, but she had no trouble recognizing Nanna in a pretty serious embrace with a man who bore a striking resemblance to Nicholai Pearce. Below the photo was a website address.

She shook her head. "I don't understand..." She glanced at Nanna, but the other woman's gaze slid away, her cheeks heated.

Of course she was embarrassed, though Flo realized she'd done nothing wrong. "Unless I'm really behind the times, it's not against the law for a widowed woman to date," Flo said.

Mayor Potts handed her an electronic notebook. "This is the article at the URL printed there."

The title of the piece was in twenty-point font and screamed across the top of the page.

"Local Businessman Accused of Swindle!"

Flo's eyes went wide. "Pearce? Is this true?"

"He wasn't charged," Nanna said, her voice sliding away as David glared down at her. "The man's a cad, Mother. I've been telling you that from the beginning. Why you insist on spending time with him is beyond me."

Nanna straightened her spine, her gaze spitting fire. "My love life is my business, David! It's none of your concern."

"It is my business when someone is threatening me because my mother is stupid enough to let herself be taken in by a grifter."

Flo held up a hand, quickly skimming the article. "It says here he romanced a much older woman and got her to give him several hundred thousand dollars." Flo looked at Nanna. "Has he asked you for money?"

Her expression tightened briefly, but she shook her head. "He has not." She turned a glare on her son. "You think I'm so repulsive Nic couldn't possibly be interested in me for myself?"

He expelled a frustrated breath. "Of course not, Mother. But, do you have any idea what my opponents will do with this in the press?"

Tears glistened in Nanna's eyes. "You're telling me you're only worried about being re-elected then? You don't care what makes me happy?"

David's frustration was clear in his face. But it was also accompanied by a fair amount of anger. He shoved his hands into the pockets of his suit pants as if afraid he'd throttle someone if he didn't. "Don't be ridiculous! Will it make you happy if this man takes you for all your money?"

"I wouldn't let that happen."

"No? Then he'll leave and your heart will be broken. Either way, you won't be left *happy*."

"You can't just assume he's guilty..."

A shrill whistle broke through their bickering, making Flo jump. Everyone turned to Agnes.

Her friend stood up, using her size to catch the fighting Potts' attention. "Everybody just needs to calm down," she told them, scowling from one to the other. "And tell us why you called Flo."

David Potts took a deep breath, closing his eyes briefly and nodding. "You're right. I'm sorry. I'm upset."

Nanna snorted, receiving a glare from her son.

"I want you to find out who sent me this," David told Flo. "If it's Pearce, I want him arrested."

Flo frowned. "Pearce? If your suspicions about him are right, why would he send you something that would interfere with his plans to coerce Nanna into giving him money?"

"It's not Nic..." Nanna started.

David's expression tightened. "Mother, even you have to admit that your judgment where he's involved isn't unbiased."

"Yes. I'll freely admit that, but hear me out. Please? I'm looking at this logically. Flo's right. Whether he has real feelings for me or not, it wouldn't be in Nic's best interests to send you that."

"Unless he's given up on you doing what he wants and figures I'm a richer mark."

"But he hasn't even intimated that he wants anything from me." She flushed, "Financially, that is."

David scrubbed a hand over his face, groaning.

Flo couldn't blame him. It had to be difficult to think of his mother dating again, never mind that he believed the man she was seeing was a player of the worst possible character. "If we assume Pearce wouldn't implicate himself, who does that leave?" Flo asked the question of both of them, but she was staring at Nanna.

"A jilted lover or an angry spouse or family member," Agnes said.

They all looked at her and she shrugged. "It makes sense, doesn't it?"

"It does, unfortunately," Flo said. She sent Nanna an apologetic look. "I'm sorry, hun. Everything I've heard about Pearce is that he's a bit of a ladies man."

To Flo's surprise, Nanna didn't argue.

"I'm guessing we start with relatives of this woman in the article," David said, frowning thoughtfully.

"That's where I'd start." Flo frowned. "I don't have the resources the police do, however."

"I'll instruct the police to dig into any further complaints regarding women," David said, tugging his cell from his pocket to make the call. "I'll tell them to give you whatever they find."

Flo nearly grinned. It was nice to have friends in high places.

"What about Sophia and François?" Agnes asked. "They definitely have reason to cause trouble for Pearce."

David walked away, barking instructions to somebody, probably one of his aids.

Nanna's eyes grew wide. "The people who own that new restaurant?"

"Yes. Apparently, he's been a bit of a problem for them in their restaurants."

"A problem?" Nanna repeated. "How?"

Flo shared what Bethany the hostess had told them.

"Do you have any proof of this?"

"No. But the hostess wasn't the only one to tell us a similar story," Flo said gently.

Nanna shook her head. "It's all lies. Nic actually told me about those people. He said they'd thrown him out of the restaurant simply because he'd complained about his food once or twice. He said they were very thin-skinned for people who deal with the public. It sounds to me like they hold a grudge too."

SILVER HILLS WAS HOPPING when they got back. As Agnes pushed through the doors, a shout of welcome made Flo jump as several of Agnes' usual party buddies hailed her from the bar.

"I'm going to have an iced tea," Agnes told Flo with a straight face. "Are you coming?"

Flo was going to decline, but she spotted Eliza Kemp sitting at the end of the bar, her head dipped close to a younger woman as she listened intently. "Sure. I could use an iced tea."

They headed for the bar. Agnes veered off to join her rowdy friends as Flo headed for Eliza.

Both the gossip queen and her victim looked up as Flo sat down.

"Hello, Flo," Eliza said, her twitchy gaze skimming sideways in some kind of manic message.

"Hi, Eliza." Flo ignored Eliza's swimming gaze and offered her hand to the woman between them. "Hello. I'm Florence Bee."

An unhappy sigh filled the air in Eliza's vicinity. "This is Margo Bleeker, Flo. She's...was...Mae's neighbor."

Ah. Flo suddenly understood why Eliza had been trying to get her to leave. The gossip queen had found a juicy source and didn't want to share the spoils. Flo gave Margo a consoling look. "Did you know her well, hun?"

Shoulders rounding, Ms. Bleeker lowered her head as if she were being beaten from both sides. Eliza must have been working her over pretty good before Flo arrived. "We weren't friends, but we spoke in passing."

"I'm sorry for your loss," Flo told the other woman.

Margo lifted her head and looked Flo in the eyes as if trying to judge her sincerity. She must have liked what she saw because she nodded. "Thank you. It's terrifying, you know? Having that happen right next door to me."

"I can imagine. Have you lived here long?"

"Only about three months." She smiled sadly. "I really like it here too. Now I suppose I'll have to move."

"Oh no, hun, don't do that. What happened to Mae..." Flo's voice trailed off. She was suddenly unsure what to say. That it was a one-time thing? They'd unfortunately had other murders at Silver Hills. Still, Flo always felt safe there. It was a good place. "We're a community here," she finally said. "We look out for each other."

"Nobody was apparently looking out for Mae," the woman said morosely.

"Would you like something to drink, Mrs. Bee?" Dutch the Bartender asked.

"Iced tea, please. With a lemon?"

"You got it." He hurried away to fix her tea.

"Mae's death was a terrible thing," Elisa told Margot. "I'll admit it has us all a little spooked. But have you noticed that everyone is paying closer attention now? Without even discussing it, we've all joined a sort of neighborhood watch. Nobody's going to get away with trying anything violent again. Not if the residents at Silver Hills can help it."

Flo had noticed people being more watchful, asking more questions. But she hadn't given it a lot of thought. She'd had her mind on finding the killer.

Margo shrugged.

"Did you hear anything that night?" Flo asked.

"Some thumping. But that wasn't unusual for Mae. She always seemed to be rearranging her furniture."

"Did you notice anybody hanging around her door lately? Anybody she might not have been happy to see?"

"Not until that night. I passed an older man carrying a box of stuff down the hall. As I was waiting for the elevator, Mae opened her door and glared out at him. She told him it wasn't a good time and that he should go away."

"What happened then?" Flo asked.

"The man argued with her. He kind of pushed the box at her until she stepped back and then followed her inside, closing the door. I got the impression she didn't want him there."

That didn't sound like Roger. "Can you describe the man?" Flo asked.

"Tall, distinguished-looking."

"Had you seen him around here before?" Eliza asked.

Margo shrugged. "Probably. I'm not sure. It doesn't matter anyway. The police have the killer in custody now."

Flo glanced at Eliza in surprise. "Do they?" Had she missed Pearce's arrest?

Eliza's eyes bugged out at the thought she might have been behind on a scoop. "Not as far as I know."

Margo sipped her wine. "Yeah, I heard they'd taken him off to jail. Roger somebody..."

Flo felt the blood draining from her face. Without thinking, she reached out and clasped Margo's wrist. "When did this happen?"

Margo shrugged, tugging her arm away. "A few hours ago."

Dutch placed the iced tea in front of her, and her gaze shot to his face. "Dutch?"

He frowned. "She's right. Mr. Attles walked out of here with the police like she said. He was escorted by Detective Peters and that big, greasy guy. I'm sorry, Mrs. Bee. I just assumed you knew."

Flo slid off her seat. "I've got to go."

She ignored Agnes calling her name as she hurried toward the front door. Heavy footsteps pounded up behind her as she reached the exit.

"Flo! Hold up. Where are you going?"

Flo shoved the door open, plunging out into a cold, Indiana night. "Roger's been arrested. I need to..."

A big hand found her arm, tugging her gently but firmly back through the door into the warmth of the lobby. "You need to what?" Agnes demanded softly. "You can't help him until we have more information."

Flo twisted her fingers together, frustration bubbling through her. The idea of Roger Attles sitting in a jail cell was making her physically ill. "I don't know. But I need to make Detective Crabby Pants see reason. Roger couldn't possibly have hurt that woman." Flo felt a sudden, irrational anger toward

Mae Caldone. She fought it with a deep breath, lifting a shaking hand to her face. "This can't be real."

Agnes pulled her into a rare hug. "Just say the word and I'll round up a gang to bust him out. I think old Mr. Klipps was in jail once. Maybe he can give us tips on how to break Roger out."

"Klipps spent an hour in a holding cell for yelling at a mounted officer because his horse pooped in the street," Flo told her friend. "I hardly think that qualifies him for a spot as leader of a prison break."

Agnes shrugged. "Still, he did hard time. Maybe he picked up some pointers from the other ex-cons."

Flo rolled her eyes.

"Flo!" Celia and TC hurried up to them, their expressions dour. "We just heard," TC said, giving Flo another hug. "You must be so upset."

"We're going to bust him out." Agnes' eyes went round as she looked at Ce. "Hey, Mass is a fixer, right?"

Celia shushed her. "Keep it down, Agnes. Mass doesn't want that to be general knowledge."

"And you told *Agnes*?" TC asked, arching a dark brow.

Celia winced. "Tactical error."

"I can keep a secret," Agnes said, frowning at her friends.

"Mass is a fixer?" Elisa Kemp said, hurrying up to them. "Why didn't I know that?"

"Apparently you do now," Celia said, glaring at Agnes.

Agnes flinched. "Sorry."

"We don't need a fixer," Flo said. "Or a plan to break Roger out of jail. We need to figure out who really killed Mae so we can clear Roger."

The door to the Manager's office opened and closed behind them. The overhead lights flickered. They all glanced up when the music in the speakers stuttered as if a rogue electrical current had sifted through the wires, disrupting it.

"Is it dusk already?" TC asked.

"I don't have my torch lit," Agnes said.

Celia patted the pockets of her slacks. "I left my pitchfork at home."

Flo sighed. "Maybe if we don't move they won't see us."

"Good E-ven-ing," a deep voice drawled. "What are you hapless villagers plotting? Scurry away now, back to your homes and gather your crosses and garlic."

They turned to find the vampiric duo of Morticia and Vladwicke Newsome staring at them with death grimaces stretched across their pale faces. The black-eyed pair hadn't spent much time moving among the "great unwashed" of Silver Hills since Vlad had lost his bid for mayor and had gone skulking into the shadows. Flo envisioned them darting out of the office to fly in bat form around the residence once everyone had gone home for the night.

"Hello, Vlad. Morty." Flo didn't bother to smile. Even if she'd felt like being pleasant, it would have been like water off a bat's back to the Newsomes.

They pretty much hated everybody.

"What's all the commotion about?" Morty asked, her narrow face and pinched lips giving the impression she'd sucked on somebody who ate a lot of lemons.

"Roger's been arrested," Agnes blurted out.

"Agnes!" Flo said, earning a narrowing of Agnes' eyes for her trouble.

"It's not like they won't find out," she told Flo.

"Is that all?" Vlad drawled meanly. "We already knew that. We thought you were gossiping about something new."

Eliza crossed long arms over her flat chest. "How did you manage to keep it quiet?"

Morticia ran blood-red-tipped fingers along the wide white stripe in her black hair. "You'll have to ask Richard. We weren't even here. Apparently, he didn't think all you snoop-dogs had a right to his father's business."

Richard! Flo turned without another word and walked away from the group, tugging her cell phone from her purse. She quickly dialed Richard's number, waiting for him to answer.

It went to voicemail after several rings. "Richard, it's Flo. I just heard. Call me back, please."

"You can't help," Vlad sneered. "I understand the police have physical evidence against Mr. Attles. It's not looking good for him."

"Plus, he's a *lawyer*." Morty grimaced theatrically. "They're all scoundrels. Everybody knows it's only a matter of time before his type switches sides of the table in an interview room."

Knowing if she stayed around she'd probably start flashing her cross and looking for a butter knife to behead the vamps, Flo stalked outside and headed across the parking lot. Behind her, the door opened and the sound of several pairs of feet followed her to her car.

TC, Celia, and Agnes all climbed in as Flo slid behind the wheel. They didn't say a word, only providing silent support as Flo started the car and headed out of the lot.

If things went badly at the Silver City Police Department, Flo couldn't help thinking they might need to trade their torches and pitchforks in for something a bit more modern. Like deviousness and determined skulking.

CHAPTER SIXTEEN

Meanie Meldick was sitting at the front desk, a sandwich as thick as Flo's arm clutched in two meaty fists. He looked up when they marched into the building and groaned aloud, mayonnaise dripping down his chin. "Not now, Ladies. I don't have time for your antics."

Flo arched a brow at that. "No time in between bites?"

Meldick swallowed hard, as if he hadn't adequately chewed his bite. "I'm on dinner break. Come back in about a week."

Agnes stepped forward and Meanie's mouth fell open, revealing the unswallowed dregs of his previous bite. TC made a gagging noise. Flo and Celia winced.

Agnes leaned toward him, her finger stabbing the air in front of her. "You listen to me, Jason Meldick, Flo's heart is breaking in two. The love of her life is singing prison ditties in a concrete room with a seatless stainless steel toilet. He's two hairs away from being sent up the river. In fact, he's probably getting a prison tat right this minute. The least you could do is let her talk to Detective Peters."

Meanie blinked as if having trouble connecting the dots between singing, seatless toilets, rapidly flowing water, tattoos, and Detective Peters. Flo didn't blame him. Agnes had really covered some ground with that one.

"I just want to talk to Brent," Flo tried. "Please tell him we're here."

Meldick hesitated another moment, looking from his sandwich to the glowering crowd of women and back to his sandwich again. On some level, he had to know he wouldn't be left alone to enjoy his dinner until he'd dispersed the angry mob.

TC cleared her throat and stepped forward. "I'd like to see Detective Peters, Jason. It's an emergency."

Meldick's small eyes went round. It was one thing to deny Flo entrance to the bullpen. But if the Detective found out Meanie had denied entrance to his girlfriend, Meanie would have crosswalk duty at the grade school for the rest of the year.

Giving a gusty sigh, he heaved himself out of his chair. "Follow me, please."

BRENT PETERS WASN'T at his desk. Meldick left them there with instructions to sit down, be quiet, and stay out of trouble.

They glowered at him as he waddled away, back to his beloved sandwich.

As soon as the uniformed officer was out of the bullpen, Celia hurried around Brent's desk and dropped into his chair, cracking her fingers before glancing at TC. "Tricia, you run interference."

"How do I do that? I don't know where Brent is?"

"Just go stand over there by the hallway leading to the interview rooms. He'll come out of there sooner or later." She glanced at Agnes. "You go stand by the door to the lobby in case Meanie tries to come back."

Agnes saluted Ce and headed quickly in that direction.

Flo came around the desk. "What are you going to do?"

Celia's fingers danced across the keyboard. "I'm going to find out what kind of evidence Peters has against Roger."

Flo felt her eyes go wide. "You can do that? I'm sure it's all password protect..." Her voice trailed away as the screen saver disappeared and an investigation record replaced it. "How'd you do that?"

Celia leaned in, reading the text on the report. "I help Mass when he needs to know what the police know. I have a gift. Turns out I'm kind of an idiot savant with computers."

"Light on the idiot part," Flo said on a chuckle. She began reading over Celia's shoulder. She quickly learned that Peters had followed much the same path as she had, except he'd dug into each of the witnesses to determine the viability of their testimony.

Celia punched a button that sent the report to Print. She got out of the chair and headed for the printer that kicked up across the room just as TC turned and gave a low whistle in warning.

Agnes hurried back to the desk. Celia stuffed several sheets of paper under her sweater and pulled her jacket over them. TC rushed back to join the three other woman.

Ten seconds later, Brent Peterson rounded the corner and stepped into the room, his stride hitching visibly when he spotted them waiting for him. He sent a glare in Flo's direction. "I can't believe you have the nerve to show your face here."

Flo didn't have to fake her surprise. "What? Why?"

The detective dropped into his desk chair, giving TC a smile and then returning his gaze to Flo with a scowl. "Siccing the mayor on me? Is that your interpretation of staying out of my investigation? Because, if it is, you might want to buy a better dictionary so you can look up the word 'interference.'"

Flo shook her head. "I had nothing to do with that."

Peters looked at his screen and frowned, his gaze sliding to each of them in turn. Fortunately, TC and Agnes could look appropriately innocent because they'd been on lookout and had no idea what Ce had done. Flo made sure to keep her expression neutral. Celia frowned back at him. "What is it, Detective? Did you want to ask us something?"

Flo nearly choked. She couldn't believe Celia's moxy.

Peters blinked and shook his head. "No. I was just wondering how long you'd been here." He very deliberately grabbed a file and slid it off the top of the desk into the large center drawer.

Flo had to fight to keep from looking at Ce. Had the information they'd wanted been right on top of the desk? She pushed past the face-palm moment and sat in one of the chairs across from the Detective. "I want to know why Roger was arrested."

Peters regarded her through a slightly narrowed gaze for a moment. Then he expelled air. "He hasn't been arrested. Not yet."

Flo let relief take her for a moment. "That's good. I'm telling you, he's not guilty, Brent." Flo rarely called the cop by his first name for fear of undermining his authority around the other cops. But it seemed like a good time to remind him he was dealing with friends. And friends of friends.

"Believe it or not, *Mrs. Bee*," he said very deliberately. "I do know what I'm doing."

She shook her head and then realized how he might take the action. "I know you're good at your job, Detective. I'm also aware of something called Occam's Razor."

He nodded. "The simplest answer is usually the correct one. I'm familiar too. That doesn't mean I take shortcuts in my investigations."

"Nobody's suggesting you do, Brent," TC said, giving him a smile.

He grimaced, his face flushing. "I don't want Roger to be guilty. But as I told you before," he slid his gaze back to Flo. "I have to follow the evidence."

"And where is the evidence taking you?" Agnes asked.

"Unfortunately, most of it points to Roger."

Flo sat forward, stabbing her finger on top of the desk. "Roger would never hurt a woman."

"I'll admit I have trouble seeing that too. But the *fact* remains," he emphasized the word fact. "...that he was found with Mae Caldone's blood on his hands. He was the only one in the apartment when her body was discovered. He's been described by the neighbor as having forced his way into the apartment..."

"She didn't describe force," Flo defended. "And she didn't describe Roger either. Just a man who could have been him."

Something like respect flashed across Peters' face. "You spoke to Margo Bleeker?"

"I did. I also talked to Bonnie Feckle, who verified that Nicholai Pearce was very aggressive and she didn't put murder past him if he didn't get what he wanted."

"I'm assuming you also spoke to Nanna Potts?"

Flo flushed, knowing he had her on that one. "I'm still not fully convinced Nanna isn't covering for him."

Astonishment lit Detective Peters' handsome features. "You think Mayor Potts' mother is lying?"

"Why not? She's human." Flo was aware she sounded a bit desperate. But it was true, a woman who fancied herself in love might do things she wouldn't normally do. "She believes Pearce is a victim when everyone else describes him as a predator." Everyone except for François Liberte.

"A predator?" Peters laughed. "That's a bit extreme, don't you think?"

"Not at all. Mae Caldone herself told me he was very aggressive in pursuing her. I saw it with my own eyes."

"Did he harm her in some way?"

Flo frowned. "Not physically, no. But Ms. Feckle said he was without scruples..."

"Did Pearce harm her?"

"No." Flo sighed.

"What about Bethany?" Agnes asked.

"Bethany?" Peters looked perplexed.

Aha! Flo thought. *Got ya.* "The hostess at Le Petite Bistro," Flo said. "She described Pearce as a man who was unhinged, who'd be willing to defame, embarrass, and even ruin the Libertes to get what he wanted. Mrs. Liberte said he was poison."

"I spoke to the Libertes. They had nothing negative to say about Nicholai Pearce."

Flo clenched her fists in her lap, frustration digging deep. "That's it? You're just going to believe everyone except Roger?"

"It's not a matter of believing or not believing, Mrs. Bee. It's a matter of evidence. Right now, the only evidence I have is against Roger Attles. I'm really sorry. I know that's not easy for you to hear..."

"I want to see him." She surged to her feet, face hot with anger.

Peters stared at her for a long moment. Flo was certain he was going to deny her demand. Then he nodded. "If he wants to speak to you, I'll allow it. But before you go in there, you should know that I've begun investigating relatives and friends of women Pearce might have mistreated..."

Hope soared. "You found something?"

"Not yet, no. But I'll keep digging. Maybe that will turn up something."

Flo deflated but gave him a nod. "Thank you for telling me."

"Of course. As usual, you assume we're on opposite sides." He stood up. "That's just not the case. I'll go make sure Mr. Attles wants to speak with you."

CHAPTER SEVENTEEN

Roger looked exhausted and beaten. He sat at the long table with his head bowed and one big hand clutching a steaming cup of coffee. He didn't even look up when Flo came into the room.

"Roger?" she said, her heart twisting painfully at his beaten look.

Without lifting his head, he said, "I almost told Peters not to let you come back."

Tears burned Flo's eyes. "Oh, Roger."

He finally looked at her. She expected to see defeat in his blue gaze. To her amazement, what she saw instead was anger. His jaw was tight and his eyes blazed with rage. "This whole thing is ridiculous, doll. I'd never harm a woman."

Flo hurried over and sat down next to him, leaning in to kiss his cheek. His skin felt hot and dry under her lips and, for a moment, she worried that he might be sick. "Are you feeling okay?"

He nodded slowly. "I'm just tired. It feels like I've been here for hours. I don't even know how long. They took my cell phone from me."

Flo glared at the mirror on the wall. The detective hadn't said he'd be overseeing their conversation, but she knew he would be. "That's barbaric. I understand you're not under arrest. How could they take your phone?" Flo imagined Detective Peters wilting under her glare behind the one-way glass. Not because she believed he would, but because it made her feel better.

Roger lifted the cup and sipped, grimacing. "I'd always believed the bad coffee thing on the TV cop shows was just a trope. Now I know it's based in reality."

Flo leaned close so Peters couldn't hear what she said. "Have you remembered anything else from that night?"

Roger slid a quick gaze toward the glass before answering in a low voice. "Bits and pieces. I remember falling backward and hitting my head on something hard." He glanced at his bandaged arm before lifting his gaze to Flo's. "I remember fingernails clawing my arm." He frowned. "Why would someone claw my arm?" His voice was filled with what sounded like genuine confusion.

She fought her own fears to give him a reassuring smile. "Do you remember whose fingernails they were?"

"A woman's. That's all I know. I couldn't tell you why she scratched me or how." He shook his head, doubt and fear making him frown. "What if I did it, Flo?"

Something flipped in her belly and the fear she'd been trying to hold at bay came roaring back, making the blood rush from her face. "I refuse to believe that, Roger Attles. And you need to reject that notion too."

But he wouldn't look at her, and the hand holding the coffee was shaking.

Flo had never seen him so distraught. "Did you call Arthur?"

Roger nodded. "He's in Chicago, but he's contacting Bruce."

Flo didn't know Bruce Benedick well. She'd met him once or twice in the halls of Silver Hills when he and Roger were heading in or out for some ballgame or other. He was a decade or so younger than Roger and, unlike Roger, was still billing hours at the firm. Though she understood he was working toward semi-retirement. "Is he a..." she nearly choked on the word but forced it past her lips, "...criminal lawyer?"

"One of the best in the country. I probably should have called him first anyway, but..."

He didn't need to finish the sentence. Roger considered Arthur a good friend. He'd have wanted a friend at his side if he was facing a murder charge.

"I'm sure Arthur will help," she told him.

Roger nodded. If the thought comforted him, he didn't show it.

"Detective Peters told me you weren't under arrest. If that's the case, you can leave at any time." She felt silly telling him that. Roger had practiced law for almost fifty years, he'd have known that.

"Yes, but if I can help, I want to stay. I'm the last person to see that young woman alive, and I might have seen the killer. If only I could remember..."

"It will come to you. How's your head?"

He laughed bitterly. "About like you'd expect."

Flo dug in her purse and came up with a small, travel-sized container of pain killers. "Take some of these. They'll help."

He took three of the small, red-coated pills and swallowed them with a swig of coffee. "Thanks, doll."

"I'm going to figure out who did this, Roger," she promised him. "It's all going to be okay."

He stared at the coffee between his hands, not responding.

Flo sat with him for close to a half-hour before Meldick entered the room and told her she needed to leave. Flo was almost relieved. Roger needed support, but she wasn't doing him any good sitting there and she had work to do.

Seeing him had made her even more determined to find a killer. Even if she had to bring him to ground herself.

FLO LEFT HER FRIENDS in the lobby, too depressed to talk or visit. She headed for the stairs at the center of the lobby, intending to climb them to her second-floor apartment. She'd take Rodney out for a final potty break and then settle into bed with a pad and pen and try to lay out the details of what she'd learned so far. The truth had to be hidden somewhere within the details. She just needed to lay it all out and find it.

Eliza Kemp's voice drifted down from above and she saw the woman start to descend the stairs, her cluster of friends slash gossip mongers clucking and flapping around her like a flock of hens.

Flo quickly changed direction and headed for the back staircase, ducking through the door into the stairwell just as the women landed in the lobby. Elisa was the last person she felt like speaking to at the moment.

She started up the first short flight of stairs and stepped onto the landing. The door below her opened on a wash of air and drifted closed with a quiet thump. She picked up speed in case it was Elisa, hitting the second short landing as the footsteps sped up behind her.

She stopped and the footsteps stopped too. Flo's pulse spiked. Whoever it was, they were trying to stay quiet. There was only one reason someone would do that. She peeked over the railing, trying to see who was following her, but saw no one. The person had to be pressed against the wall to stay out of sight.

Heart pounding in her chest, Flo started up the steps again, going as fast as she could.

The footsteps behind her sped up, moving even more quickly than Flo.

She ran faster, tripping once as her weary legs started to complain about the pace.

The footsteps behind her came faster, hit the treads harder, no longer going for stealth. Her pursuer cut the distance between them faster than her feet could move.

Flo was panting for breath by the time she reached the door to the hallway on the second floor. With a sense of relief, she reached out and grasped the handle, tugging it hard and wondering if she could make it to her apartment and inside before her pursuer caught up to her.

Steps slowed below her as if the person following her thought they'd lost the race.

But Flo quickly realized that wasn't the case at all.

The door wouldn't open.

She tugged again but it didn't budge.

With a jolt of horror, she realized that someone had locked it from the outside.

Flo glanced upward, wondering if she could make it to the third floor and get to Agnes' apartment before the person in pursuit caught her. Her heart pounded and her breath heaved through her lungs, painful in its intensity.

A figure rounded the landing below and started toward her.

In desperation, she glanced up the stairs, even taking one step in that direction.

"Don't bother, Mrs. Bee," a familiar voice said. The man climbed the final short rise of stairs toward her, his face hidden under the shadow of a baseball cap. She recognized the tall, lean form, elegant and graceful like a stalking tiger.

"What do you want?" she asked Nicholai Pearce. But she was very afraid she knew exactly what he wanted. And it wasn't going to turn out well for her.

He stopped two steps below the landing and looked up, the weak light of the stairwell finally finding and illuminating his coldly attractive features. "What do I want? I want you to stop trying to pin a murder on me." The threat in his voice was real. It was a sharp bark beneath the seemingly reasonable tone. It was evident in the stiff jaw and the lightly fisted hands hanging at his sides.

"I'm not trying to pin anything on you, Mr. Pearce. I'm simply trying to find a killer. Do you have something to hide?" Flo could have kicked herself for taunting him. It was foolhardy and very well might end in her being thrown down a flight of stairs.

Or worse.

The man was clearly enraged and not doing a very good job of hiding it.

To her amazement, he smiled. It was a mean smile, but with it, his jaw relaxed. "I have a lot of things to hide, Mrs. Bee. I would have thought a smart woman like you would have figured that out by now. I don't really want the police or the news shining a light on my life."

"I understand. Cockroaches tend to scatter when you shine a light on them." *Stupid Flo. Stupid, stupid Flo*, she scolded herself silently.

He climbed the final two steps and hit the landing, taking two long strides so that she had to step back to put some distance between them. He loomed over her, rage glittering in the depths of his eyes under the ball cap. "Mind your own business, you stupid cow. I didn't kill that woman. Your friend Roger killed her. The sooner you own up to that, the better off you'll be."

Flo swallowed hard, pressing her back against the door to gain another inch of space. She tried to remember if she had any mace or anything useful as a weapon in her purse. She might have a small can of hairspray. Her gaze locked on his, Flo slipped her fingers into her purse, talking to distract him from what she was doing. "Mae told me she wanted to break up with you. I saw you fighting with her on the sidewalk in front of Le Petite Bistro. You couldn't stand that she was rejecting you, so you killed her."

Her fingers slid over her wallet, her cell phone, and a pack of sugarless chewing gum. They pressed into a stack of tissues and skimmed over her keys. But no hairspray. Where was that dang hairspray?

Pearce's fist came up, stopping inches from her face as he ground out a response from a clenched jaw. "You don't know what you're talking about."

"Don't I?" Her fingers touched something smooth, cylindrical and she clasped them around it, tugging it free from the tissues. "Then why don't you tell me where I went wrong?"

"I didn't care about Mae. She was the one who was obsessed with me. She accused me of flirting with every woman I met."

Flo clutched the cylinder in her palm, turning it slowly and feeling for the spout. It wouldn't do to spray herself in the face. "Well? Isn't that what you do? You flirt, charm, and cajole until you get what you want. And if that doesn't work, you simply threaten."

He laughed. "Sometimes, yes. I've been known to use charm. But I'm a man who gets what he wants. I won't apologize for that."

"And if you have to use force to do it?" She felt the rough area of the spray nozzle and rested her finger on the top, ready in case Pearce tried anything.

He shrugged. "I don't know. I've never had to use force." His grin was feral, threatening.

"According to the hostess at Le Petite Bistro, you tried to ruin them to get what you wanted."

He laughed. "The woman's delusional. She can't stand that I wasn't into her."

Of all the arrogant... Flo nearly rolled her eyes.

"I came to Silver City to get away from those people. Liberte broke into my apartment and painted stuff all over my walls with red spray paint. He's crazy. They all are."

Surprised by his statement, Flo wasn't sure if she believed him. Her fingers tightened on the hairspray. "You're saying they threatened you?"

"Not that it's any of your business, but yeah. Liberte accused me of trying to sleep with his wife. Somebody put a bug in his ear."

"Did you?"

Pearce chuckled, shaking his head. Flo didn't get the sense he was denying the charge, only amused by it.

"Are you blackmailing Mayor-elect Potts?"

Pearce appeared to be caught off guard by her question. He blinked once, his brows lowering as his eyes narrowed. "What are you babbling about now, woman?"

"Someone sent a blackmail letter to the mayor. It included photos of you and Nanna Potts together. Did you send it?"

Pearce settled back on his heels, giving Flo some much-needed space. His face softened as he smiled, clearly relaxing. "Why would I do that? Nothing good is going to come to me from that."

"Unless you're hoping for a bigger payout from the mayor than you stood to gain from his mother." Flo's neck hurt from the tension in her shoulders. She needed to have her head examined for accusing Pearce of blackmail on top of everything else.

"Blackmailing the son of the woman I want to get close to would be stupid. I'm not a stupid man. Despite what you seem to think." Without warning, Pearce leaned nearer, his hot breath bathing her face. "Stay out of my business."

"Or what?" she asked, wondering to herself if she'd lost her beady little mind. The very last thing she should be doing was provoking a potential killer.

He opened his fist and tucked a finger under her chin, forcing her head up so she was looking him in the eyes. "You don't want to find out."

Then the painful pressure on her chin was gone, and she was watching his back as he descended the steps. He stopped at the landing and turned back. "By the way, I wouldn't tell the police about our little conversation if I was you. Your friend Roger has been a very bad boy. I have evidence to prove it. You don't want me to release that evidence to Detective Peters. He's a very enthusiastic cop. He'd feel the need to do something about it if I did."

Flo leaned against the door, her chest heaving with terrified panting as she listened to his no-longer-stealthy footsteps descending toward the first floor. She didn't move until she heard the door open and close. Then she took off running as fast as she could to the third floor, where the door, thankfully, was unlocked.

Flo took the elevator down one floor and hurried into her apartment. A moment later, she called Agnes and asked her to come over. She needed to take Rodney out for his potty break, but she didn't want to go outside alone. Her encounter with Pearce had left her shaking.

CHAPTER EIGHTEEN

When Agnes arrived, Flo opened the door and grabbed Rodney before he got his teeth on Agnes' sneaker.

Agnes glared at the cranky senior doxie, curling her lip at him when he showed his teeth. "I don't understand why your dog hates me," she told Flo.

Flo grabbed her arm and tugged her into the apartment. "Nicholai Pearce just confronted me in the stairwell."

Agnes' eyes went wide. "Seriously?"

Flo nodded. "The man's a psychopath."

"Speaking of psychopaths..." Agnes handed Flo the sheets of paper Celia had copied at the station.

"You read through Peter's report?"

"We all did. It looks like Pearce is on the detective's radar too. Look at the section on Bonnie Feckle."

Flo's eyes went wide. "The soap lady? Has something happened to her?"

"I assume she's fine. This happened a few weeks ago. Apparently, someone broke into her apartment and spray-painted threats on her walls."

Pearce's revelations about a similar experience played through her mind. "Pearce complained about the same thing. He blamed François Liberte for it."

"Why would Liberte threaten the soap girl?" Agnes asked.

"More importantly, why was this event documented in Peters' report?"

"Because she blamed Pearce. She claimed he'd been trying to strong-arm her into letting him partner in her business."

No wonder Ms. Feckle wanted to move to a new place. The young woman had downplayed Pearce's aggressiveness to her. Flo quickly read through the report and glanced at Agnes. "I need to talk to her again."

Agnes nodded. "You need to tell Detective Peters about Pearce attacking you."

"I can't." Flo's stomach twisted as she remembered Pearce's threat. *Your friend Roger has been a very bad boy. I have evidence to prove it.*

"Can't?" Agnes asked. "Why not?"

Flo shook her head, unwilling to tell Agnes what Pearce had said about Roger. She couldn't bear for anyone to think for even a minute that Roger was guilty. "That's not important. Just trust me, I can't tell him."

"Okay, but the information might be enough for Detective Crabby Pants to arrest the man."

Flo winced. Agnes was right. She sighed. "I'll call Peters and feel my way through it. Maybe he's already planning on arresting Pearce and I won't have to tell him."

Agnes moved past Flo. "You have any cookies?"

"In the cookie jar. I made them yesterday. Peanut butter."

"Yum!" Agnes said, grinning as she headed into the kitchen.

Flo moved into the living room and scanned the report as she waited for Peters to come on the line. When he did, his tone was gruff, unfriendly.

Pretty much business as usual.

"Yeah?"

"Detective Peters, I was just wondering how the investigation's going?"

There was an angry pulse of silence before he spoke. "It would be going better if I wasn't spending hours of valuable time digging up all of Nicholai Pearce's old flames."

"Oh? Do you think Pearce is a real suspect?"

"My opinion of his guilt or innocence hasn't changed. I'm simply complying to your buddy, the mayor's *suggestion*, which I'm pretty sure came from you. Why are you asking me that now?"

"No reason."

"Mrs. Bee, I know you well enough to know when you're digging for something. What's up?"

She bit her lip, still reluctant to tell him about Pearce. But in the end, she saw no way around it. "Nicholai Pearce accosted me in the stairwell tonight."

A taut silence pulsed through the line. "Accosted? Are you all right?"

"I'm fine. He didn't hurt me. But he threatened me multiple times. He accused me of sticking my nose in his business."

"You're not actually offended by that, are you? Sticking your nose into people's business is kind of what you do. It's your reason for living. Your specialty. Your favorite pastime. Your fondest hobby..."

"Okay, I get it. Don't beat a dead horse."

"But seriously, he didn't hurt you?"

"Not physically, no. But I'm pretty shaken up. It made me hope you had something on him that would make you arrest him."

"There might be something."

"What?"

"I can't tell you that, Mrs. Bee. It's an ongoing investigation."

She sighed, biting her tongue against asking if it was the Bonnie Feckle thing. She couldn't let him know she'd read his report. He'd have porcupines *and* kittens if he found out. "Can you at least tell me if it's likely he'll be brought in for questioning?"

"Brought in for questioning, yes. In fact, a couple of uniformed officers are on their way now to do just that. But arrested? I just don't know yet. And I wouldn't tell you if I did."

"Okay. That's fair. Thanks, Detective Peters."

"I don't need to tell you that this just got too dangerous for your further involvement, do I?"

"No. You don't need to tell me that," she said evasively.

He sighed. "But it wouldn't matter if I did, would it? Be careful, Mrs. Bee. If Nicholai Pearce *is* our murderer, he's already not happy with you. When we bring him in for questioning, he's going to be as mad as a wet hornet."

And he was going to assume Flo was behind the questioning. Worry roiled sour and hot through her stomach. Pearce would waste no time revealing the "secret" he claimed to have against Roger. If he had one at all. Anything to point the finger of blame toward someone else.

With that realization, Flo's worry turned to real fear. "I'll be careful."

He disconnected without another word, leaving Flo to brood about the way things were shaping up. All signs pointed to Pearce. He had the temperament, the opportunity, and the motive.

Murders were generally motivated by three things: Love, money, or revenge.

In Pearce's case, Flo could make a case for all three of them.

So why didn't it feel like he was guilty?

"Theshe are delishiosh," Agnes slurred around a mouthful of cookie.

Flo turned in time to catch a moist crumb on her cheek, grimacing as she scraped it off. "Detective Peters is bringing Pearce in for questioning."

Agnes swallowed. "That's great! Hopefully, they'll let Roger go now."

Flo didn't bother to set Agnes straight on Roger's situation...his voluntary incarceration at the Silver City PD. She simply nodded, deep in thought.

Her cell rang and she looked down at the unfamiliar number. She almost hit the *Ignore* button and then changed her mind, punching the *Answer* button instead. "Hello?"

"This is all your fault."

Flo sat for a moment, digesting the accusation and trying to place the voice. "I'm sorry?"

"This. You brought this on me again. I'm soree now that I talked to you."

The faint accent and the unique pronunciation of the word sorry finally made it click into place. "Sophia? What's wrong?"

"I left all my friends behind. My family. And came to this 'orrible place," the woman on the other end of the call took a shuddering breath. And still, I must deal with this."

Flo stood up and grabbed her purse. "Are you talking about Pearce? Has he hurt you?"

Sophia sobbed quietly. "He won't stop until I'm dead. Like that woman, Mae. He's going to kill me." She was sobbing quietly into the phone, sounding terrified.

Flo motioned toward the door and Agnes followed her out. "Sophia, have you called the police?"

Sniffling. "No. I need to speak to François."

"Call the police and then call your husband. I'm coming right over. Lock all the doors and watch for us." Flo didn't wait for the other woman to respond. She disconnected and redialed the police department.

"What's going on?" Agnes asked.

"Sophia Liberte's been threatened in some way. She's too upset to tell me what's going on, but I think she was talking about Pearce."

The phone stopped ringing. "Silver City Police Department."

"Mean..." Flo managed to stop herself before she called the uniformed cop by the moniker they used behind his back. "Officer Meldick, I need to speak to Detective Peters again."

They trotted down the stairs, Flo not wanting to wait for the elevator, and hurried through the lobby. Voices called out to them but Flo didn't slow or look. She barreled as quickly as she could toward the door.

"He's not here. You want to leave a message?"

She shoved the door open, a blade of icy air stabbing her in the face. "No. I need to speak to him. Can you give me his cell phone number?"

"Nope. Not allowed."

She bit back frustration. "Then give him mine, please. We have an emergency. Mrs. Liberte just called me and she's very upset. She believes Nicholai Pearce is going to kill her." Flo realized she was filling in a few blanks that she maybe shouldn't, but she couldn't think of any other "he" who might be threatening Sophia. Then she remembered what Peters had said earlier. "Do you know if they brought Pearce in for questioning?"

"Tall guy, silver brown hair, granite jaw?"

Flo's stomach twisted with alarm. "That sounds like him."

"Yeah. He's sitting in interview right now. And boy is he mad." Meanie chuckled. "If his eyes were daggers there wouldn't be a cop left standing in this building."

Flo disconnected and slammed her car door, glancing at Agnes in the passenger seat. She appeared to still be chewing cookie. "Pearce is at the police station."

Agnes swallowed. "Then how did he threaten Mrs. Liberte?"

Flo thought of what Pearce had said. The painted threats on his apartment wall. Then she realized what had been bothering her.

The details fell into place and she knew everything. She knew who'd killed Mae Caldone and why. And if she was right, Sophia Liberte was in terrible danger.

CHAPTER NINETEEN

The guard wasn't in the gatehouse when they arrived. His golf-cart-type vehicle was missing too. Flo assumed he was driving around the neighborhood.

"I'll hit the button for the gate," Agnes said, jumping out of Flo's car. But she came back disappointed after trying the door and finding it locked.

Dang the man for being a conscientious guard. Although, Flo hoped that meant the person who was stalking Sophia couldn't get inside the neighborhood either.

"We'll have to go over the fence," Agnes said, rubbing her hands together with anticipation.

Flo eyed the eight-foot-high stone fence that surrounded Grandwood Estates. "Unless you have a ladder in your pocket, we're not going over that fence."

Agnes rolled her eyes. "Where's your sense of adventure, Flo?"

"It's with the ladder we don't have." She shook her head. "*You* might be able to climb that fence, but I know my limitations."

"I'll give you a hand up. It will be fine," Agnes said with unrealistic confidence.

"I don't think..."

"Let's at least try it, Flo. I'm cookie-fueled. I feel like I can do anything." Agnes' teeth gleamed in the glow of the security lights shining down on them from the guard shack.

Shaking her head, Flo motioned toward the street. "Let me park under that tree there, so if the guard comes back he won't have my car towed."

A few minutes later, they were running along the fence, looking for a good spot to try to scale it. They found a place where there were a couple of chipped rocks the size of one of Agnes' thumbs, and she insisted the spots would be big enough for her to use as toe holds.

Flo eyed the tiny cracks, certain Agnes was being overly optimistic. "I don't know, Agnes..."

"It will be fine. Go stand facing the fence and stretch your arms up as far as you can. I'll hoist you up to the top and then all you have to do is slide down the other side to the ground."

Flo's eyes went wide. "Slide down? I don't like the sound of tha..."

Before Flo could finish voicing her concern with Agnes' plan, two strong hands jerked her leg off the ground and encircled the bottom of her foot.

"On three," Agnes said.

Flo leaned into the wall, her heart pounding with fear. "What happens on three?"

"...two, three!" Agnes straightened her knees and Flo flew upward, screeching as she landed on top of the fence and hung there, her legs dangling, feet kicking.

"Okay, just dig your toes in and shove," Agnes said from down below.

"Are you crazy?" Flo asked, fighting to pull herself onto the six-inch-wide top. "I'll slide over and land on my head."

"Here, I'll help." Agnes shoved on the bottom of Flo's shoes, sending her over the top of the fence on a scream. Flo's head hung three feet down the inside of the wall, her boohind stuck up to the moon, and her feet flailed the other side in a panicked attempt to gain purchase. Flo's head started to throb as all the blood rushed into it. "I'm stuck!" she yelled at Agnes. "I can't go forward and I can't come back."

"Hold on," Agnes said in an unconcerned voice. "I'll be up there in a snap."

Flo stared down at the next problem, realizing she really didn't want to fall face-first off the wall. "Agnes, there are rose bushes planted along the wall as far as I can see."

"Umph!"

Flo heard the meaty sound of Agnes' sturdy body hitting the wall. "Are you okay?"

Silence met her question. Flo tried to twist around to see her friend, but there was no way she could lift herself that high. "Agnes?"

"I think I broke something."

"Just great," Flo murmured. She was going to be stuck hanging there with her wide butt in the air until the guard came back and found them. The humiliation might kill her. "You need to help me get down."

Agnes groaned. "It really hurts, Flo."

"Can you just hobble over here and tug gently on my legs?"

"I'll try."

The thrashing sounds below and behind Flo reminded her of a herd of rhinos charging through the underbrush.

"Umph!"

Something brushed Flo's leg. "I've got the toe hold," Agnes yelled, her voice triumphant. "I just need to...argh!"

A hard hand wrapped around Flo's ankle and Agnes yelped, her body smacking hard against the rock wall and what felt like her entire weight hanging off Flo's leg.

"Ahhhhhh!" Pain jolted up her leg and into Flo's hip, becoming best friends with the agony cutting through her middle as the edges of the rock wall sliced across her body. "Let go!" she shouted to Agnes.

But Agnes was kicking against the wall, trying to grip something with her sneakers. "I've almost got..." An extended grunting sound preceded another thump, another "umph!" and suddenly Agnes' hand was clawing its way up Flo's calf.

Fingernails dug into Flo's flesh through the fabric of her slacks. Her stomach felt as if it was being cut in half.

Fortunately, though, her leg was turning numb, which Flo figured was going to be bad in the long run, but saved her some agony in the moment.

A hand landed on Flo's butt cheek. She straightened with a yelp of surprise, her head lifting a foot off the surface of the wall. "Agnes!"

"Sorry! Man your butt is scrawny. It's hardly enough to grab."

"Agnes Willard, I am not a climbing wall. Get your hand off my butt cheek right this minute."

Agnes stilled and the night grew silent as Flo realized just how loudly she'd screamed that last.

She could only imagine what the neighbors were thinking if they'd heard it.

Fortunately, Agnes' hand stopped molesting her and slapped down onto the top of the wall. A moment later, her friend's sweaty, bright red face appeared above the fence. Agnes dragged herself onto the wall and turned around, sitting with a leg on either side. "Why don't you sit up, Flo. That doesn't look very comfortable."

Flo bit her lip to keep from screaming. "It's not very comfortable. In fact, it's downright agonizing. Especially with you climbing me like a tree."

"Let me help you sit up," Agnes grabbed one of Flo's arms and jerked, whipping her around and nearly off the other side of the wall.

Flo screamed again and grabbed Agnes' beefy arm. "Good Lord, woman! Do you not have a gentle setting?"

"Sorry," Agnes said. "I always forget you weigh about as much as my purse." She helped Flo ease around until she was sitting astride the fence facing her. "Now what?"

Flo glanced down. "We can't jump down here. We'll land in those rose bushes."

"I don't care if we smash a few flowers, Flo. A woman might be in danger."

Flo didn't need the reminder. It made her pulse spike. "It's not the flowers I'm worried about, fool. It's us. There are thorns all over those bushes."

Agnes frowned. "Oh, yeah. I guess we could try scooting closer to the gate. It looks like maybe there's an area there that doesn't have bushes."

Flo didn't like that plan, but she didn't have a better one. "Okay. I guess that's our best option." Then she realized she would have to turn around. "You'll have to give me a minute while I turn around so I can see where I'm going."

"No problem. Here, let me help..."

Flo yelped as Agnes grabbed for her leg and tugged, unbalancing her on the wall and tipping her sideways. With a terrified shriek, Flo lost her seat on top of the wall and plunged downward.

Into the thorny rose bushes.

LIMPING DOWN THE STREET, Flo rubbed at her cheek, grimacing at the sharp pain her touch caused.

"Um," Agnes said sheepishly. "You have a little thorn..."

Flo glared at her friend, slapping Agnes' hand away as she tried to pluck the offending thorn from Flo's cheek. "Leave it be. You've done quite enough."

"I said I was sorry."

Flo snorted angrily. "One of these days, you'll be apologizing over my grave for shoving me out of a plane or something. Note to self," Flo said sarcastically, "Don't stand near any open doors or windows in an airplane with Agnes."

Agnes expelled a sigh. "Okay, putting that unpleasantness behind us..."

Flo narrowed her gaze but didn't remark.

"What's the plan with Sophia? Do we just march up to the door?"

Flo's gaze slid toward the large contemporary home ahead of them. The oversized windows were dark, and the façade was cold and uninviting. "I'm not sure. We'll just have to figure it out when we get there."

Agnes pointed toward a small vehicle in the driveway of the Liberte's home. "Is that the guard's golf cart?"

Flo nodded in relief. "It looks like it." Sophia must have called him. That was good. "We'll just check in real quick and be on our way." Despite her words, something felt wrong about the scene ahead of them.

Agnes nodded. As they walked, silence fell between them and Flo felt Agnes' regret in that silence. She finally reached out and looped her arm through Agnes', giving it a squeeze to show her friend she didn't hold a grudge.

Agnes squeezed back, her steps growing lighter.

They were walking up the sidewalk to the front door when Flo realized what had been bothering her. "All the lights are off."

Agnes nodded. "Maybe she went to bed." She glanced at the watch Hertz had given her for her birthday and frowned. "It's only nine o'clock. But some people go to bed early."

Flo nodded. She never went to sleep that early, but she liked to climb into bed to read at around seven. However, she wouldn't do it with a neighborhood guard at her house. "With the guard here?"

"You have a point," Agnes said, her voice lowering.

The front door opened under Agnes' knuckles when she knocked. They shared a look and Flo whispered, "We'd better call the police."

Agnes pointed toward the glass in the door. "What's that?" Someone had scribbled something across it in what looked like white soap. Flo couldn't make out the words, they were gibberish. Then she realized why, pulling the door open and reading it from the inside.

You're dead!

"That's not good," Agnes said.

Flo opened her mouth to respond but never got the chance.

A hand snaked through the door and grabbed her arm, yanking her none-too-gently inside the house.

CHAPTER TWENTY

"Ah...!"

Agnes came through the door like a ninja, arms flailing and feet set wide on the tile, knees bent. "Who's there?"

"Shhh! What are you doing here?"

Flo recognized Sophia Liberte's voice and turned around, seeing the woman's indistinct shape in the dark. "We came to check up on you. It sounded like you were in danger on the phone."

Sophia expelled a sigh.

Agnes swung a belated fist, the air whooshing past Flo's ear at the narrow miss. She slapped out at Agnes' arm. "Stop that! You almost boxed my ear."

"Will you two be quiet, please?"

"What's going on, Sophia?" Flo asked, growing impatient.

"I don't know. But I'm pretty sure somebody took out Carson."

Flo frowned. "Carson?"

"The guard at the gate. I called him when my lights went out. He came up my driveway and parked that little car he drives, then I heard him shout once, and I've heard nothing since."

"Why was your front door open?"

"I'd just been calling quietly for him, considering going out to check on him, when you ladies showed up."

"Why don't we lock up and turn on the lights," Agnes suggested.

"Good idea, hun." Flo patted Sophia's arm. "Then you can tell us what's going on here."

"Please do lock the door," Sophia said. "But the lights won't come on. I've tried that already."

"Where are the kids?" Flo asked.

"Staying with friends, thank goodness. François had to go to Indy. We had a break-in at La Délicatesse. Somebody trashed the kitchen."

"Oh no!" Flo shook her head. "That's a shame."

"Yes. And now this. I'm starting to feel as if we're under attack."

"I don't blame you, hun. Would you like to come stay with me tonight? I have an extra room."

Sophia shook her head, the moonlight through the window creating shadows under her eyes. "I'm not leaving my house."

"Well, if your suspicion about the guard is correct, then you're in danger here."

Sophie lifted her hand. Flo grimaced when she made out the shape of a gun. "Nobody's going to hurt me. And if they try they'll eat my steel."

Flo didn't correct her. She was pretty sure bullets weren't made of steel. "Well, you won't be able to defend yourself in the dark. We need to get the lights on."

"Where's the breaker box," Agnes asked.

"In the basement. But you'll need a flashlight to get down there. The stairs are steep. I think there's one in the kitchen drawer."

They made it to the kitchen with minimal bloodletting and only moderate bruising. Plus, Agnes might have taken out an end table, Flo was pretty sure she heard cracking wood when Agnes' muscular knee plowed into it.

By the time Sophia found the right drawer and turned on an oversized flashlight, Agnes was limping as badly as Flo.

The arc of illumination from the flashlight flared weakly over them and faded, flaring again as Sophia smacked it with the heel of her hand. "Stupid thing. It never works."

She handed it to Agnes. "That's the door to the basement." She picked up the gun she'd set on the counter while she searched. "I'll stay up here and keep an eye out the window while you two try the breakers."

Flo wasn't thrilled leaving Sophia alone, but she couldn't talk the woman out of it, so she and Agnes headed downstairs. Halfway down the steps, the flashlight went out.

Agnes pounded on it and it flared briefly, held for two steps and then went out again.

Flo heard clicking noises. "Hit it again," she said helpfully.

Agnes hauled off and smacked it so hard it flew out of her hand, bounced off the unpainted drywall and clattered down the steps.

They stood in stunned silence for a moment. Then Flo sighed. "We're dead center. It's pitch black at the top and pitch black at the bottom. Which way do you want to go?"

"Up. Even if we make it downstairs, we won't be able to find the box without at least a little light."

Flo nodded, realizing Agnes wouldn't see her. "Okay, I guess we'll feel our way up the steps then."

Flo grabbed the railing and felt around with her foot, trying to find the next step. When she did, she slid her foot until it was fully supported and stepped up. It was slow going but Flo was deathly afraid of taking another tumble. She was lucky she hadn't broken something important falling off the wall.

She didn't want to test fate with another fall.

By the time they felt their way halfway to the door, Flo heard voices. She stopped and threw out a hand to stop Agnes. But Agnes couldn't see it and she plowed right into Flo, sending her sprawling ungracefully across the next step up.

"What was that?" a woman's voice asked.

"Probably the cat," Sophia responded in a shaky, breathless voice.

"That was a pretty big cat," the woman said, and Flo heard footsteps heading toward the basement door. She grabbed Agnes' hand and gave it a warning squeeze. Unfortunately, they had nowhere to go. They were pretty much trapped unless they wanted to risk a hurried retreat down the darkened stairwell.

A tall figure appeared above them, only faintly painted into visibility by the moon shining through the kitchen windows.

The moonlight also illuminated the unmistakable shape of a gun clutched in her hand.

Had she overwhelmed Sophia and grabbed her gun?

The woman stood there for a long moment, peering into the darkness as if she could see Flo and Agnes, and then seemed to decide she'd imagined the sound and retreated, closing and locking the door behind her.

They were well and truly trapped.

"Well, crap," Agnes breathed.

"We need to try to unlock that door," Flo whispered.

"We can't go barging up there. We don't know who that was," Agnes said. "Did you hear Sophia's voice. She's scared. That might be the person who took out the guard."

"Okay, then. What do you suggest?" Flo asked.

"Let's make our way downstairs. Maybe I can coax a few more minutes of life out of that flashlight. Then, if we're really lucky, there'll be a window or an exit of some sort down there."

It was as good a plan as any. Better than Flo's desperate option of throwing themselves in front of the woman with the gun. "Let's go."

By the time they made it to the bottom of the stairs, voices were raised above their heads, and a series of crashes culminated in the sound of something heavy hitting the floor.

Something like a body.

"We need to hurry up," Flo told Agnes. "I think Sophia's in trouble."

A shot rang out above them, followed by an ominous silence.

Flo tugged on the back of Agnes' shirt. "Let's move. We need to split up and double our chances of finding the breakers."

"Wait!"

Flo hesitated mid step. "What?"

Agnes moved closer, lowering her voice. "Did you bring your phone? We could use the light on that to see where we're going."

Flo felt her pockets, then remembered she'd left it in her purse. "No. Dangit! It's in the car." Flo gave Agnes a hopeful look. "You?"

"I didn't grab mine before we left." Agnes sighed.

Flo shook her head, the brief hope dying. "I'll head right. You go left."

Agnes' only response was a swishing of fabric and the scuff of her shoe on the floor.

Flo stretched her arms out in front of her and started a shuffling walk, listening carefully for any sounds from above, or anything in the room where they were that might give her a clue where she was headed.

With her vision all but gone, Flo's other senses started to kick in. She noticed the utter silence first. The lack of power was complete, it appeared. Nothing was running. There was no sound of water working its way through a softener system. No sound of a heater kicking on or warm air soughing through ducts and airways.

Nothing but stark, unending silence.

Clang!!!!!

Flo jumped a foot off the concrete. "What in the world?"

"Sorry," Agnes' voice came from across the room. "I think I just found the washer and dryer."

Flo took a deep breath, trying to still her pounding heart. If the person with the gun was still upstairs, Agnes' banging in-to the laundry appliances would have told her in no uncertain terms that they were down there. They needed to find a way out of that room, and fast.

"I think there's a window up here," Agnes said in a harsh whisper.

Flo turned around and headed toward the sound of Agnes' voice. "Can we get to it?"

"If we climb up onto the washer..." An ominous buckling sound wrenched the silence. "I think I'm too heavy. You're going to have to do it," Agnes said.

"Of course I am," Flo murmured. Her forward progress crashed to a halt as her head bounced off something metal with a soft, concussive *booonnnngggg*.

Pain ratcheted through her neck and knifed down her spine. A silvery array of stars danced before her gaze. Flo's hands snapped out to find the object she'd run into, discovering something tall, cylindrical, and rough to her touch. A metal support pole. Probably rusty, which would explain the roughness.

Rubbing her forehead, Flo stepped around the pole and spread her arms out, fingers splayed and thumbs touching in the center so nothing could escape her early warning system.

She heard Agnes' breathing a few seconds before she reached her. A beat later, her hands found something soft and squishy.

"Hey, that's my boob!" Agnes objected.

"Now we're even for you feeling up my boohind at the wall."

Agnes chuckled. She grabbed one of Flo's invasive hands and placed it onto the cool metal of either the washer or dryer.

Flo's gaze was actually starting to acclimate to the full dark and she could see the outline of the appliances.

"I'll give you a boost," Agnes offered.

Flo lifted a hand. "Not a chance. You'll fling me into the window or the concrete wall. I'll do this myself." She lowered the hand and felt around until she found a round indentation in the front of one of the appliances. She felt for the handle on the dryer door and yanked it open.

Something hit the floor above and footsteps trailed overhead.

"Hurry, Flo. It sounds like she's coming this way."

Flo stepped on the inside of the dryer door and shoved herself upward, her knee finding the surface of the dryer. When she stood straight, She was looking into the black rectangle of a small window. Beyond the glass, moonlight provided the only illumination beyond the glass. Someone had killed all the street lights in that part of the neighborhood.

Flo fought with the latch on the window. "This is either rusted or someone's painted it over."

Agnes bent double and came up with her shoe. "Hit it with this."

Flo grabbed the offering and turned back toward the window, readying the shoe.

Something hit the glass on the other side, and a terrified face peered in at her.

Flo screamed and scrabbled backward. She nearly fell off the machine, but Agnes gave her a shove to keep her from plunging to the floor. Flo hit the concrete block wall with a soft, "Umph!" sound as her mind belatedly recognized the face in the window..

Overhead, footsteps thumped in their direction.

"It's Hertz!" Flo said, whacking the latch hard with Agnes' shoe. She tried turning the latch again and it moved a little, so she whacked it a few more times.

The lock turned and Flo tugged the window open. "Hertz! What are you doing here?"

He reached for her hands. "No time to explain. Let me help you out. You're in terrible danger."

The door at the top of the stairs slammed open. "Who's down there?"

Hertz yanked Flo's arms and dragged her through the window, the narrow frame scraping painfully against her sides and hips as she narrowly made it through, Hertz dropped her in the cold grass and turning back to the window. He stuck his head through. "Come on, Agnes."

"I'm not going to fit through that window," Agnes said. Her voice was filled with fear as a small arc of light started down the stairwell toward her. "Just get Flo out of here and call the police."

"I'm not leaving you," Hertz said, his tone determined.

Behind Agnes, there was a scream and the sound of something heavy bouncing down the steps. The arc of light swirled around the room and went out as the flashlight clattered against the floor.

"She's down," Agnes whispered. "I'll just stay out of her way until Detective Peters gets here. Now go!"

The window slammed closed in Hertz's face. He swore softly, handing Flo his phone. "Call Peters. I'm going in after Agnes."

In that moment, Flo realized that Hertz Thomson loved her friend. She felt deep gratitude for him and gave into an impulse to give him a quick hug. "Agnes is very lucky to have you."

He shook his head. Flo couldn't see his expression, but she heard the love in his voice when he responded. "I'm the lucky one. Now hurry. Agnes is in terrible danger."

As if to prove his words, a gunshot went off inside the basement.

And Hertz took off running toward the front door.

CHAPTER TWENTY-ONE

"Agnes!" Flo screamed, panicking. She smashed her face against the window, trying to see her friend. "Are you okay?"

Something shifted through the darkness, a large form moving fast toward the stairs. "Watch out!" Agnes yelled.

Flo ducked just as a bullet pinged off the window frame and shattered the glass, spraying Flo's arms and legs in millions of tiny shards of glass.

Flo landed hard on her bum in the grass, stars bursting before her gaze as she realized how close she'd come to being shot.

And then bursting anew when she realized Agnes was still in danger.

A siren roared toward them through the night. "Hold on Agnes! Help's coming."

There was a loud grunt, the sound of flesh hitting the concrete, and the slam of a door as somebody, presumably Hertz, threw the basement door open.

A narrow beam of light flared on and sifted down the steps, bathing Agnes and the woman she battled in weak light.

Heavy footsteps pounded toward them.

The woman fighting Agnes started to turn, the hand clutching the gun swinging toward Hertz, and Agnes gave a primal yell, like the scream of an avenging Amazon warrior, and threw her considerable bulk at her combatant.

They went down with a clatter and crash, the gun going off in a burst of light, and Flo heard wood splintering nearby.

Hertz appeared at the bottom of the steps and kicked the hand holding the gun, sending it flying. "Agnes!"

"I'm fine," Agnes told her panicked rescuer.

Hertz sagged to the steps, his wide face tense in the cast-off glow of the flashlight. "Thank goodness. I think I lost ten years of my life."

Agnes lay atop the struggling woman, who was moaning with pain and clutching her hand to her chest. "You broke my wrist!" she lamented in a whiny voice.

"Good!" Agnes said.

Someone staggered toward Flo. "Ma'am, you need to stand back." The man's words were slurred as if he'd been drinking. He fumbled for the gun on his hip. "I called the police."

Flo turned to the man, whom she finally recognized as the guard from the gate. He was holding his head and moving unsteadily.

She hurried over. "The woman's been subdued and disarmed. Here..." she said. "You should sit down before you fall."

He allowed her to help him sit in the grass, groaning softly. "She snuck up on me. Pistol-whipped me."

A Silver City police car roared down the street and whipped into the Liberte driveway, screeching to a halt. The door flew open and Meanie Meldick struggled out of it, panting and sweating in the flashing lights of his police unit. He leaned on the roof and focused the gun in their direction. "On your bellies, arms and legs spread wide."

Flo rolled her eyes. "We're the good guys, Jason. The gunman is inside. Agnes and Hertz subdued her. But somebody needs to check on Sophia Liberte, and this man needs an ambulance."

"I don't need..." The guard started to shake his head but stopped, retching into the grass as his skull no doubt fought back from the movement.

Another police unit and Detective Peters' unmarked sedan roared up and parked, the cop car's headlights slashing across the lawn and highlighting Flo and the downed guard.

Peters jumped out of his car, much more limber than Meanie had been, and yelled at Meldick to stand down. He sent the two uniforms in the second unit into the home, their guns drawn.

Peters hurried over. "Has he been shot?"

"Pistol whipped," Flo responded, pushing to her feet. "We need to check on Mrs. Liberte."

Peters held out a hand to stop her. "I'll do that. You stay out here." He looked down at the guard. "I've called for a bus."

Flo knew "bus" was cop for ambulance. "Agnes and Hertz are in the basement. They disarmed the woman with the gun."

Peters' handsome face tightened. "They could have been killed."

Flo shrugged. "It wasn't a conscious decision, Detective. It was her or us."

He sighed. "Stay put. I need to talk to you."

Flo watched him run toward the house, gun drawn, tension tightening her muscles painfully.

"You look as bad as he does," Meanie said in his usual clumsy way.

Flo looked down at herself and realized she was bleeding from several places. Maybe the pain wasn't from tight muscles, after all. "I'm okay."

The ambulance tore up the street and rocked to a stop at the curb. All around them, neighbors had come out of their homes and stood shivering on their porches and lawns, watching the show.

Meanie called out to the EMTs, pointing them toward the guard. "Take care of him and then look at her." He turned away and headed inside the house to help Peters.

The two medical personnel, a man and a woman, hurried across the lawn toward them, pushing a gurney.

Peters came out of the house, supporting Sophia Liberte with an arm around her waist. He helped her sit down on the front step. She had blood running down her temple and her face was white. "Need some help here."

The woman EMT hurried over and crouched next to Sophia, shining a light into her eyes and asking her questions.

Peters went back inside.

Flo limped over to the basement window, finding Meanie, sweaty and panting, clapping cuffs onto the gunwoman.

Someone had found the right breaker and the lights were back on. For the first time, Flo got a good look at the culprit.

Bethany Vitter

Though Flo had expected it, the reality still surprised her.

Agnes and Hertz stood away from everyone else. Their heads were close and they seemed to be having an intense conversation. Agnes was frowning, her body language tight as if Hertz were telling her something she didn't want to hear.

Flo desperately hoped Hertz wasn't breaking up with her. If he was, his timing was terrible and his judgment suspect.

And she was personally going to box his ears when she got hold of him.

THEY SAT IN THE DINING room at Silver Hills, the sounds of Cook and her staff prepping for breakfast behind the swinging door.

Peters looked exhausted. He'd been up all night dealing with the aftermath at the Liberte home. He sat next to TC, his shoulders round and his eyes shadowed. "Bethany Vitter admitted to killing Mae Caldone. It appears it was a simple case of jealousy. She'd heard Mae and Pearce arguing outside of Le Petite Bistro and Pearce telling the victim he wanted to be with her."

Flo couldn't believe it. "All of this was jealousy?"

"Afraid so," Detective Peters said.

"A crime of passion," she shook her head. "It's so sad. Mae didn't even want Pearce. She'd been trying to break up with him."

"What about the other women?" Agnes asked. "That soap lady and Sophie?"

"Bethany believed Pearce was interested in them too. Apparently, Vitter and Pearce used to date when they lived in Indianapolis. When he broke it off she became unhinged with jealousy. She created several scenes in the restaurant and he stopped going there. Soon after that, his apartment was vandalized."

"Like Bonnie Feckle's place and Sophia's house."

Peters nodded.

Flo frowned. "Bethany said the Libertes moved to Silver City and opened Le Petite Bistro to get away from Pearce, but he followed them here."

"Actually, Pearce was here before they came. And according to Sophia Liberte, they came to Silver City at Bethany's suggestion. The Libertes were surprised to find Pearce here when they opened their doors." Detective Peters frowned. "That day you ran into me at the restaurant and I said I was working?" Peters told them.

They nodded.

"I was there because there'd been some trouble at La Délicatesse. One of my buddies on the IMPD asked me to keep an eye on Liberte. He'd taken out a huge insurance policy on the restaurant a week after they had a small kitchen fire. They'd later learned the fire was arson. There had been a few other incidents that made the IMPD think Liberte was milking his insurance."

"Bethany?" Flo asked.

Peters shrugged. "That's for the IMPD to figure out. The area where their other restaurant is located has changed. It's not in the nicest neighborhood anymore. Liberte was apparently just reacting to the run of seeming bad luck. Trying to protect their investment. It is possible that Bethany was creating chaos in the hopes the Libertes would throw up their hands and be open to suggestion. If it was Ms. Vitter who caused the incidents, her machinations probably made it possible for her to persuade the Libertes to move to Silver City. She wanted to follow Pearce."

"Sophia Liberte hated Pearce," Agnes said. "She told us he was poison."

The detective nodded. "Yes. Because she believed their longtime friend and hostess when Bethany told them Pearce was the cause of all the problems at their Indy restaurant. She poisoned the couple against him." He chuckled darkly. "Sophie Liberte needs to keep an eye on problems closer to home. Her husband has a roving eye of his own. The only difference is he doesn't seem to be leaving a trail of conquests behind him."

Flo thought about Cook's report of seeing François flirting with Bonnie Feckle. Sadness filled her at the thought that Sophie's problems might not be fully behind her. She could only hope recent events would scare François Liberte straight.

"So, what really happened in Mae Caldone's apartment?" Hertz asked. "Do you know?"

"I remembered more about what happened that night," Roger said.

They all looked at him.

He shrugged. "I remember hearing fighting behind the door when I knocked. Ms. Caldone answered the door. She had a bruise on her cheek and she looked scared, but she wouldn't tell me what was wrong. She kept looking over her shoulder and shaking like a leaf. I was worried for her. I admit that I pressured her to let me inside."

"That's what the neighbor saw," Flo said, relieved. "She said you forced your way inside."

Roger winced. "Forced seems like too strong a word. But I wouldn't take no for an answer. I knew that young woman was in trouble."

"What happened then?" TC asked, leaning forward with interest.

"I went into the kitchen and started to set the box of china down as someone stepped out of the living room with a gun. I let go of the box and it fell, shattering on the floor." He frowned as if mourning the loss of his heirlooms. "With the other woman's attention on me, Ms. Caldone must have thought she had a chance to grab the gun, and the two of them struggled over it. I tried to help and was flung back. I fell into the table, but I remember feeling something scratch my arm as I fell. I think I got caught by somebody's fingernails."

Peters nodded. "You did. And it made clearing you of the murder very difficult."

"Luckily, I had the world's best detective helping to clear my name," Roger said, grinning at Flo.

Peters snorted, shaking his head.

"Is Sophie okay?" Flo asked.

"She fell trying to avoid being shot and hit her head against a cabinet. It probably saved her life, but she'll have quite a headache for a while."

"I can attest to that," Roger chuckled.

"I don't think they'll be sticking around here, though," Peters said. "She seems to blame Silver City for their troubles."

"Their troubles came from Indianapolis," Hertz said, frowning. "It followed them here."

Agnes nodded. "I'll be disappointed if they leave. I really like that restaurant."

"Was Bethany responsible for the threatening note to Mayor-elect Potts?" Flo asked, drawing several startled gazes. She realized she hadn't had time to tell her friends about that.

Peters nodded. "She called into work saying she couldn't come in. She told François that her mother was sick and then followed Pearce and Nanna Potts to Indy, snapping pictures of them together. She knew that, if her plan worked, there was a good chance the restaurants would close down. Bethany needed an exit strategy. She figured shaking down an heir of the Potts wealth would take care of her when she became unemployed." Peters gave Roger a look, narrowing his gaze. "The big secret Pearce claimed to have on you?"

Roger nodded, not appearing surprised. Pearce had apparently made good on his threat to squeal on Roger.

"It was that Mae had told him she was afraid of an influential man in Silver City. A lawyer." Peters' smile held a tinge of relief. "He didn't get that quite right. Mayor Potts definitely has some control over law enforcement in Silver City. But he's not a lawyer. Pearce apparently assumed that would be the last nail in your coffin."

Roger shook his head. "He might have been right if you hadn't figured it out."

Flo closed her eyes for a beat, her chest loosening as the pieces came together. "Mae told Mayor Potts that Pearce was courting his mother, didn't she?"

"She did," Peters agreed. "And the mayor was none too happy about it. He kind of took the bad news out on the messenger. Mae had just been trying to warn him of the potential dangers of the relationship, for both him and his mother. She left the meeting feeling as if she'd made a powerful enemy."

"But all that happened was that the mayor eventually called a lunch meeting with Pearce, which just happened to be at Le Petite Bistro." Flo shook her head. "Probably inspiring Bethany's plan to break up Pearce and Nanna and get herself a nice payday."

"I'm surprised she didn't try to kill Nanna too," Agnes said.

Peters shook his head. "She knew that would draw too much attention to her activities. Potts wouldn't have rested until his mother's killer was found. Bethany couldn't risk that. So she settled for the next best thing. Breaking them up and putting Pearce under just the type of spotlight he hates."

"Well, that's that, then," TC said, nodding. "Another mystery solved." She beamed up at Brent and then winked at Flo.

Hertz cleared his throat. Flo glanced his way. Sitting next to Agnes, Hertz was frowning and so was her friend. Flo suddenly remembered her intention of speaking to Hertz about his plans for Agnes. Attempted murder had unfortunately gotten in her way.

She sincerely hoped she wasn't too late.

Hertz gave Agnes a smile and she flushed. He grabbed her hand and looked around the table. "If we're done with the ugly stuff...?"

Detective Peters nodded. "I'm done."

"Good," Hertz said. "Because Agnes and I have an announcement."

Flo's stomach jumped with alarm. Surely he wouldn't announce their breakup to everyone?

But Agnes' round face split in a happy grin. "We're getting married!"

The table erupted in joyful whooping. Agnes' friends wrapped around her in a happy group hug. Hertz accepted several hugs and a couple of manly handshakes. "It was like trying to negotiate a global peace accord," he chuckled. "But we got 'er done!"

Flo shook her head. She suddenly understood what had been bothering Agnes. She'd been struggling with the decision to marry after being single for her whole life.

The kitchen door swung open and Cook stuck her head out. "Is it time?" She seemed to be addressing Hertz.

"It's the perfect time," he told her, beaming.

Cook came into the room with a large layer cake, a cluster of sparkly silver candles burning in the center. She set it down in front of Agnes. Natasha hurried up behind her with a large knife, silverware, and plates.

"A cake?" Peters looked at his watch. "It's eight o'clock in the morning."

TC elbowed him. "Stop talking. There's never a bad time for cake."

Agnes clapped her hands. "Is this...?"

Cook nodded. "Caramel delight. If dis don't work, you jus' let me know. I have several other flavors I'm dyin' ta try out on ya."

Hertz laughed at their incredulous faces. "What better way to celebrate our engagement than by taste-testing our wedding cake."

"Economy of planning," Flo said, laughing.

Agnes grabbed the knife and started slicing huge pieces. "Who's going to be first?"

All hands went up. Everyone let themselves succumb to the joy of sugar and fat for breakfast. And nobody was surprised when Agnes smashed the first piece into Hertz's deliriously happy face. And then tried to lick it off, claiming she didn't want to waste it.

The End

IF YOU ENJOYED **Love Hertz**, you might want to check out the rest of the series. Please enjoy Chapter One of **Flo Charts**, Book 1 of the *Silver Hills Cozy Mysteries:*

COME TO SILVER HILLS. Where new friends are made and a grim reaper is born.

Agnes Willard is moving into Silver Hills. She's worried about the change and concerned about fitting in. Luckily for her, Florence Bee has decided to take Agnes under her wing.

When Agnes' cat Tolstoy escapes as they're getting Agnes settled into her new apartment, they quickly find him across the hall, perched on a dying woman's chest.

The new friends soon learn three things from the experience:

1. The cat definitely has an instinct for and proclivity toward people who are on death's doorstep. 2. Finding and avoiding a killer is a really tough way to spend your first days in a new place.

And 3. Agnes truly does have a unique talent for debauch-ing a crime scene.

CHAPTER ONE

Florence Bee stood in the side yard of the Silver Hills Senior and Singles Residence and watched the small moving truck pull to a stop near the front door. She was always happy to see new people moving into the Residence. It hadn't been that long ago when she was new herself.

Her dog Rodney, a slightly overweight red-haired dachshund, leapt on a hapless grasshopper as it attempted to hop on by. He danced happily around to grin at her, skinny tail wagging wildly, with the poor bug hanging out of one side of his mouth.

Flo grimaced and turned her attention back to the van.

Nobody had climbed out yet. She wondered what the person inside the cab was doing.

She'd moved to Silver Hills eight months earlier, when her husband Hank had succumbed to a gas bubble gone wrong. More properly called an air embolism. She'd been a bit out of her comfort zone for a few weeks after the move, not knowing anyone and having to learn to live in an apartment rather than a house with a sizeable yard and neighbors who kept to themselves.

Nobody kept to themselves at Silver Hills. And those who tried were socially beaten about the head and shoulders until they capitulated.

She'd learned to share her life with approximately 200 other people of all ages and temperaments. It had mostly turned out well. Though there were a few whose irritable presence Flo could do without. She generally liked only positive influences in her life, believing that negativity was aging to the soul.

The driver's side door finally opened and a large woman with a graying brown pageboy and shoulders as wide as a linebacker's lumbered out and closed the door. She stood in the drive and looked up at the building, her wide face filled with tension. Despite being close to six feet tall and probably weighing over two hundred pounds, the woman looked a little lost.

Flo felt an instant affinity for the other woman. It hadn't been all that long ago since she'd been in exactly the same position. She tugged Rodney's leash. He'd been rolling around on his back, growling happily, but he leaped just as happily into movement as Flo headed toward the van.

The other woman turned a worried face toward Flo as she approached. Flo gave her a welcoming smile. "Good morning." She offered her hand. "I'm Florence Bee. My friends call me Flo."

The newcomer shook her hand, nearly crushing it in her big, meaty paw.

Rodney growled long and low and the hairs on his back lifted warily.

The woman gave Rodney a wary glance and then shifted her gaze to the cab of the truck. A wide, orange face popped up in response to Rodney's growl and the fat, striped cat hissed in his direction.

"I'm Agnes Willard. That's Tolstoy."

Flo nodded. "He's a handsome boy."

"Thanks." Agnes Willard said, finally smiling.

"You're moving in today?"

"I am." She frowned as she responded.

"When is your help arriving?" Flo hated to pry, but she had a funny feeling that Miss Agnes Willard was more alone than she'd originally thought.

Agnes shrugged. "It's just me."

"Oh, hun," Flo said, shaking her head. "That won't do at all."

Agnes blinked rapidly, clearly surprised by Flo's attitude. "It's okay. I'm strong."

"I'm sure you are. But I don't care how strong you are, you can't lift a couch or a dresser by yourself."

"I'll be fine." The other woman's tone was dismissive. Clearly, she didn't like Flo's interference. But Florence Irene Bee was nothing if not determined and she had no intention of letting the poor woman try to move into Silver Hills all by herself. She reached out and patted Agnes' hand. "I'm sorry. I know I'm being pushy. I don't mean to be, really. It's just that...well...here at Silver Hills we take care of each other. It's like one great big family."

Agnes seemed to be thinking about that, her bushy eyebrows lowering over a gray gaze. Finally, she smiled. "I'm an only child. I think I'd like a couple hundred brothers and sisters."

Flo laughed, deciding she was going to like Agnes Willard. "You might hold that thought until you meet some of them. There are definitely a few crazy aunts and uncles in the mix."

Agnes' grin widened.

"Come on, Agnes. Let's go find you some help."

FLO WAS TEARING DOWN the final box hours later when Agnes stumbled heavily into the room, her round face filled with panic. She wiped her dusty hands on her pants as she stood. "Is something wrong?"

"Tolstoy's missing."

Flo tried to show a calm front but, judging by her new friend's demeanor the news was not good. "Surely he wouldn't go far."

Agnes frowned. "It's a new place and he's not familiar. He could easily get lost."

Flo patted Agnes on a widely made but surprisingly firm arm. "No worries. We're self-contained here. He can't get outside unless someone lets him out and the residents know not to do that. We don't have a lot of pets here but we have enough that there are rules of behavior."

Agnes nodded her head but she didn't look convinced.

"Come on. I'll help you find him."

Agnes gave her a tight smile. "Thank you."

"What are friends for?" Flo grinned back.

They headed out of the apartment as two of the young people from the Singles side were walking away, chatting about going out that evening. Flo briefly envied them their youthful energy. After hours of unpacking Agnes' stuff, she was ready for a quick shower and a night in bed reading her latest favorite mystery.

"Thanks for your help," Agnes called out.

The two women turned. The shorter one, with a head full of bouncy blonde curls, gave Agnes a thumbs up. "Come on down later for happy hour. We'll let you buy us a beer."

Agnes' plain face lit up. "It's a deal."

As the two women wandered off, Agnes and Flo looked up and down the hallway. "Where should we start?" Agnes asked with a frown.

"Off with you, beast!" a strident voice screeched.

Flo grimaced, pointing to the open door down the hallway from which the irritated shout had emanated. "That would probably be a good place."

They headed toward the open doorway and knocked on the frame.

An ancient voice, rich with cranky indignation called out. "Well come on in. You don't expect me to get up and walk all the way out there do you?"

Agnes lifted her dense brown eyebrows and Flo shook her head. "Mrs. Peoples. She's old and hates everybody," she whispered.

Agnes nodded.

They found the cranky octogenarian in the bedroom of the apartment, sitting in a recliner with the footrest lifted. She was scowling toward the bed, where a woman with straight, strawberry blonde hair lay pale and listless, her hazel gaze focused on the fat, orange cat stretched out on her belly.

Despite Mrs. Peoples' obvious disgust at having the cat in the room, the clearly ill woman in the bed seemed pleased. She was stroking his soft belly as he stretched and purred loudly enough to be heard by the door where Flo and Agnes stood.

"There you are, you little devil," Agnes said, moving quickly toward the bed. "I'm really sorry," she told the bedridden woman. "We just moved in and he apparently decided to go exploring."

The woman smiled. "Don't apologize. It was nice having him visit. What's his name?"

"Tolstoy." Agnes scooped the big cat gently into her arms, giving him a kiss on his wide, striped head. He growled softly and nipped one of her fingers but he must not have bitten down hard because Agnes didn't seem to notice. "If you'd like I can bring him back for a visit."

Flo got a warm bloom in the vicinity of her heart at Agnes' offer. She smiled, knowing suddenly that her new friend would fit in just fine at Silver Hills.

"I'd like that, thank you. I'm Betty Marlowe." She reached her hand across the bed and Agnes took it, giving it a squeeze.

"Agnes Willard. It's nice to meet you."

Flo approached the bed. "You're not feeling well, Betty?"

The woman shook her head, licking dry lips. "Something apparently didn't sit well from lunch."

"I'm so sorry. Can we bring you some crackers, maybe a lemon soda?" Flo asked.

Betty nodded toward the nightstand and an open box of saltines. "Mrs. Peoples brought me crackers. But thank you."

A long, drawn out snore drew everyone's attention to the birdlike eighty-eight-year-old in the recliner. She slept with her head back and her mouth wide open, sawing logs like a lumberjack.

Betty chuckled. "She was going to give me a soda too but carbonation doesn't sit well with me."

Flo nodded. "Is there anything else I can do for you? Shall we call Dr. Bambast?"

Dr. Bambast was a Silver Hills resident who'd retired from his practice a couple of years earlier and liked to stay busy, so he volunteered his time at the residence as sort of a first responder. He took care of simple ailments and injuries and sent the residents off for anything beyond that.

Betty shook her head. "I'm sure that's not necessary. I don't want to bother him."

"Well, if you change your mind. Just give me a call okay?"

"I will. Thank you, Flo." She shook her head. "What a week. I guess it's true that bad things do come in threes."

"Why? What else happened?" Agnes asked.

"First my boss died yesterday and then a careless driver ran me off the road on my way home from work."

"Oh my," Flo said, frowning. "Did you get hurt?"

"No. I'm fine. But my car has a nice dent in it, courtesy of that big elm tree in the park."

Flo's eyes went wide. "You're lucky you weren't seriously hurt."

"I know. I'm choosing to consider it a blessing," she sighed.

"I'm sorry to hear about your boss. How did he die?"

Betty frowned. "I don't know, specifically. They're keeping it really quiet at work and the office manager encouraged me to stay home today. He even asked if I'd brought my current project home with me so I could get some work done while

I was here. He's thoughtful that way." She pointed toward the nightstand and Flo saw the manila folder beneath the crackers. "Between you and me, I think there was something...off...about Mr. Carey's death though."

"Why do you say that?"

"The police were here, asking me all about his friends and stuff." She frowned. "They wanted to know my whereabouts for the previous night too."

"That isn't good," Flo said.

"I thought it was a bit strange."

"But you didn't ask why?"

She shrugged. "I figured if they wanted me to know they would have told me."

Flo frowned. It seemed hard to believe that Betty wouldn't even ask about her boss' death. But she had known people who just weren't curious. She'd had an aunt who'd been like that. Aunt Virginia never seemed to care about anything outside her little sphere of knitting, daytime shows, and baking.

Flo had never understood that mindset.

"And now I'm sick." Betty shook her head, then succumbed to a bout of coughing that shook the bed with its violence.

Flo handed Betty the glass of water on her nightstand. "Here, hun. Drink some of this."

The water helped ease the coughing and poor Betty fell back against her pillows after handing the glass back to Flo. She was so pale, with large purple circles under her glassy eyes. Flo patted her hand. "I'll check in on you later, okay?"

Betty nodded, her eyes closing. "I'm just going to rest..."

Flo and Agnes left the room, closing the door behind them. A loud grumbling sound from the vicinity of Agnes' round belly made Flo blink in surprise. Agnes looked embarrassed when Flo glanced her way. "I'm starving. For some reason I'm craving spaghetti with garlic toast."

Flo chuckled. "I know just the place. You get Tolstoy settled and I'll go take my dog, Rodney out for a potty break. Then I'll take you to my favorite Italian restaurant."

CHECK OUT THE ENTIRE series here: https://samcheever.com/books/#SilverHills

WHAT'S NEXT?

Read More of Sam's Work: Did you enjoy the book? If you'd like to read more books like this from Sam Cheever, check out her other bestselling books:

Silver Hills Cozy Mysteries: https://samcheever.com/books/#SilverHills

Country Cousin Mysteries: https://samcheever.com/books/#Country

Gainfully Employed Mysteries: https://samcheever.com/books/#gainfully

Grave Theatrics Mysteries: https://samcheever.com/books/#grave

Enchanting Inquiries Mysteries: https://samcheever.com/books/#enchanting

Provide Reviews: If you enjoy the books, please consider showing support for Sam by leaving reviews so that other readers will know what to expect from a Sam Cheever book. Book reviews help readers as well as authors!

Connect: If you'd like to stay up to date on Sam's News, Releases and Appearances, consider liking her Facebook Page, following her on Twitter, and signing up for her Newsletter:

Newsletter: https://samcheever.com/newsletter/

Website: https://www.SamCheever.com

Blog: https://samcheever.com/blog/

Facebook: https://www.facebook.com/SamCheever-Author

Bookbub: https://www.bookbub.com/authors/sam-cheever

Goodreads: https://www.goodreads.com/author/show/1812031.Sam_Cheever

ABOUT THE AUTHOR

USA Today and Wall Street Journal Bestselling Author Sam Cheever writes mystery and suspense, creating stories that draw you in and keep you eagerly turning pages. Known for writing great characters, snappy dialogue, and unique and exhilarating stories, Sam is the award-winning author of 100+ books.

To learn more about Sam and her work, visit her at one of her online hotspots:

Website[1] | Facebook[2] | Goodreads[3] | Blog[4]

---

1. http://www.samcheever.com/

2. https://www.facebook.com/pages/Sam-Cheever-Author/102117321982

3. http://www.goodreads.com/author/show/1812031.Sam_Cheever

4. http://samcheever.com/blog